THE MIRROR OF THE GIANT

By the same author

ALL THE USUAL HOURS OF SLEEPING
WAILING MONKEY EMBRACING A TREE
RAINSPLITTER IN THE ZODIAC GARDEN

THE MIRROR OF
THE GIANT

Penelope Shuttle

MARION BOYARS
LONDON · BOSTON

First published in Great Britain in 1980
by Marion Boyars Publishers Ltd
18 Brewer Street, London W1R 4AS

Australian distribution by Thomas C. Lothian Pty Ltd
4-12 Tattersalls Lane, Melbourne, Victoria 3000

© Penelope Shuttle 1980

ALL RIGHTS RESERVED

ISBN 0 7145 2679 7 (cased edition)

Any paperback edition of this book whether published simultaneously with, or subsequent to, the cased edition is sold subject to the condition that it shall not, by way of trade, be lent, resold, hired out, or otherwise disposed of, without the publishers' consent, in any form of binding or cover other that in which it is published.

No part of this publication may be reproduced, stored in a retrieval system or transmitted, in any form or by any means, electronic, mechanical, photocopying, recording or otherwise, except brief extracts for the purposes of review, without the prior written permission of the publishers.

Type set in Great Britain by
Gloucester Typesetting Co. Ltd., Gloucester.
Printed by
The Anchor Press Ltd, Tiptree, Essex

ONE

SHE moves from room to room in the semi-dark of the house. Torn maps direct her journey.

Some nights she kept herself hidden, very secret, unavailable, lost in a sisterhood he could not understand. Some nights she spent annulled in the orchard, beneath the awkward appletrees. Some nights she waited in a blind alley of flowers.

On other nights she watched him as he slept. She says to Theron,

'A wife is walking towards the sea and a wife perceives the night unsteadily.'

Tonight she is silent. She looks through mist and rain. What she eats tastes like pieces she has ripped from god's body, and the flesh is sour as toads. Her long heavy hair drags her down like a sea. She is icebound but she hears summer calling her. The penis of summer is tempting her but she is silent. She stands by the window, the night moves restively about her.

Her name is Vellet.

In the morning, he studies his books in silence. He is tired. Last night he slept badly, alone, in a dusty room. On his desk, in a silver frame, is a photograph of his late wife, Vellet. He glances at her stilled smile and he wishes for peace. He wishes to be free of her. He wants her zodiac to close its mouth. But I'm being swallowed up, he thinks suddenly, in a panic, and looks around the room, harshly.

Beth woke up, afraid. Fear like an aromatic taste in her mouth, a taste like apples of earth. It was early in the morning but he was already up, maybe practising the art of beautiful handwriting or perhaps mending the garden fence. She sat up in her barbed-wire bed and realized that her life in this place, with Theron, was undesirable to her, alien in every way now. But every solution, every escape that she conjured up in the first light of morning cancelled itself out: the noise in the background of milk churns being loaded on to the delivery lorry derided her with an every-day practical competence that she could not find in herself. She saw again all the difficulties of change, renewal, and her own weakness drove her back into familiar impairment. Rain tapped on the window. Sadly and unwisely she slept again. Her dream went on hurting.

In the middle of the field, a scarecrow covered in fatal feathers is waiting for her. But she runs away, and not for the first time. Her luminous shadow pleased him as he watched her running. He stands at the crossroads. When she saw him, she slowed down and walked towards him reluctantly. Bleak as scripture, the sky darkens. The man and the woman converse about honesty and cannot agree. Your womb is a nutshell, Beth. She sees the ghosts of her retina, pale seaport creatures. Love slips away through the eye of a needle.

TWO

BETH is alone in the pensive room, recovering from a minor attack of influenza she caught wearing her new summer dress for a cold May Day, a shivery celebration. This morning she sits at her white table, painting flowers on a square sheet of glass.

Her husband Theron enters the room. He knows that this is the day of her ovulation. It seems to him that his wife is gradually being lost to his view, that she is a careful mirage he might erase by using the wrong password. He stands in the doorway, deliberating. But she misinterprets his watchfulness and shouts angrily, 'leave me in peace! Let me have a calm day alone! I don't want you hovering on the outskirts of my thoughts.' She sends him away with all her strength. And in the room huge rippling circles of solitude remain to intimidate her. 'Don't play your bloody tricks on me,' she shouts after him down the passageway. He does not answer. She leans against the door, full of grief and anger.

That evening Beth and Theron go for a walk. The moon is murmuring like a pleased domestic animal. Beth stares at Theron, chilled to a little smile that tells him nothing. He grabs her arm and pulls her towards him. The moon reminds Beth of all wives and children. White faces. 'What about the time when you pretended to be dead?' he asks her. She trembles. 'You and I must go our own ways, it isn't working out, there's a wall between us a mile high, two miles wide.' He smiles. She looks more closely and sees the mudstains on his shirt. 'Separate?' he says calmly. 'No. You are the one I have chosen, Beth.'

She looks around her, at field, stream, stone and tree of twilight. She hears the night beginning within herself. He led her home, like a nun approaching the cold cage of holy week.

Brain-tissue of the night. All that night the idea of Vellet's body dragged up on to the river bank, ornamented with bracelets of weed and necklaces of jetsam, all night the thought shuddered through Beth, the night was made unbearable by her own feeble cries for help, her own drowning.

All night she was drenched in elvish sweat. Alone in the dark she thought of Vellet.

Vellet's ghost is tall and wet by the side of her bed and is swathed in the damp colours of Vellet's enmity: night reflected in the bedroom mirror, drowning there.

Vellet, beast-girl, first wife, five years dead. White skull of the girl who has charge of Theron's insomnias bends over Beth, functionless breath of Vellet chokes Beth. Beth carries the remains, the scars of the day with her into a restless shallow sleep.

Without a coat, Theron walks out of the house, into the fields. He is determined upon retaliatory action. He heads for the river.

'It is easy for you to reproach me,' said Beth, 'it is easy to confuse me.' That morning he had given her a long list of her faults. She shook her head. Theron, there are splinters of worlds under my fingernails. They hurt me.

They walk in silence through the forest. Beneath their feet raw pale loppings from the branches are the proof of last night's storm.

A midwife is singing somewhere. The song tells Beth that she can be freed from her self-made sadness. But Beth is not listening. Theron is speaking to her. On their way home from their afternoon walk they loiter by the town cenotaph. She's picked a bunch of marsh andromeda from the river bank and at home she puts the flowers in a vase, governs them badly. Theron compliments her on them. She smiles at him. For a time it seems the dangers were exaggerated.

THREE

BETH is waiting for a letter from Ash. Darkness strikes the land forcibly, the moons damage Beth, the unmanageable afternoons come back. In the morning she expects a letter. Every morning. But no letters come. It is no fun, this waiting. It is like an unalterable distance which must be travelled every single day. A silent toxic journey.

Beth, housewife of calamities. For Beth the walls of the house are a prison. She appoints Theron her warder. He has no choice in the matter. She blames him for her own submissions. He is the man who carries fire and laws in his hand simply because Beth says so. Beth says so because Ash will not write to her.

My antagonist changes sex, says Beth. Reptilian mirrors coast me back to the dark. My antagonist changes sex. Theron/Ash. Ash/Theron. He/She/Elohim walks in the woodland of the scissors. And who will ambush me there?

White rainbows will be my downfall.

But the reflection of a spider in a raindrop saves me from the depressions that are threatening. The alternating colours return, the world returns, with its suns and salts, I return to myself, even though I remember how the ghost rotates in her wetness. She gleams with her lifeless smile, with her wintry lace of drowning. She is his companion, she is the wife. I must listen to her legends. When once again there is no letter I sense the beauty of the electric-chair, I know the splendour of the gas-chamber. The dream-road shines then and Vellet offers me the day before yesterday. She whispers: 'God will dissolve your marriage, despite his crown of petals, his broken mirror.' But I return to myself, despite my unhappiness. I return to myself, not to Vellet. If Ash has forgotten me, then I'll occupy that devastation of myself with a purity, not with Vellet's stench creeping in upon me.

Vellet leaned forward and whispered in Theron's ear: 'The wife of Harlequin just kept lying there in the mud, laughing and slaking her sensitive flesh in the mud: Harlequin said, be careful, remember your clothes, they'll get so dirty. The mother of Harlequin's wife stood on the river bank, watching, her face made impassable by the rains. Her gestures were without speech, required none.

'Harlequin's wife got up from the mud and her long hair was stiff, like the black snakes of Egypt. Her shadow was composed of a flock of black cuckoos.

'Harlequin offers her the bunch of red flowers. She smiles, she is shivering. She is naked now, having abandoned her muddy skirt and blouse at the river's edge. Her husband wraps her in a tartan blanket and the trio enter their winter conveyance to drive off along the highway . . .'

FOUR

THE kiss that Beth and Ash exchange explodes into morning and beyond the dream Beth's exterritorial life begins. Shivering in the cold bedroom, she dresses hurriedly and goes downstairs to prepare breakfast, thinking of her dream. Around the neck of the goddess hung painted skulls. The goddess was set in a niche in the wall and her draperies were stone. The stone goddess had Ash's face. The skulls are the skulls of her lovers. I fish for them, and draw them up in a white net. Or was it that the skulls dangled from my long silvery tapering fishing rod? One skull grows flesh and features, smiles at me, it is Ash also.

Where is the giantess in her iron dress? Where is the giantess holding up a mirror, her hands encased in gloves of bronze? I have not seen her yet. He said to me: 'Beth, let the darkness enter your heart.' I cannot forget Jake's words. Jake stands between us, Ash. I can never forget that.

I know I am not the inventor of the firmament. My fears spread out beyond me like branches. I am a tree of sadness and constant winter.

Theron came in and sat down. They ate breakfast in silence until over a second cup of coffee, Beth said,

'When I was a young girl, first experiencing my monthly issue of blood, then I was fully alive, truly responding to all things. Every day was the day of the moon. Every night was an arena of sunshiny dreams. But now I am flung from day to day like a beggar, owning nothing. The whirlwind is too strong for me. My agile ancestry cannot go that fast. Now I want to live on the sheltered side of the east wind.'

'I want to help you,' said Theron gently, stroking her hair, 'but you frighten me, Beth, when you stare at the household furniture like a wife murdered a century ago.'

'I sense a power in me,' she said, after a moment, 'a source of strength and freedom deep within me, but I cannot reach it, gain access to it. I cannot mine the treasure. I do not know the password to enter that region. And ever since I sensed this power, soon after our marriage, I have become awkward in all my actions, clumsy emotionally. The part of me that knows that power is there, presses against the remainder of my life, demanding entrance. But I do not know how to let it in. That power leads to an equilibrium of abilities. With it, I can come into focus and find peaceful solutions to my problems, a detente. But I am afraid. And I stare at the furniture like a wife murdered a century ago.'

Theron shrugged and sighed, and left her in the kitchen. She thought, Ash is my reflection. Her light to my dark, her dream on my day, her answer to my question.

Ash walks in a landscape hundreds of miles away, beside wild Lent lilies flowering by another river bank.

Yet we both shrink back from the looking-glass, flinch from that reflection. Lady Unique: that is how I think of you, Ash. I see you on stairways, in rainy fields, in your herbarium: echo of me, my reflection, receding always, no longer turning to me, to see your reflection in me, always retreating. Yet my need for you will not die down or lessen. It is like an inheritance. I was marked for this from the day I was born. Only you are free, Lady Unique, dancing without hesitation among your children. Heroine, who has led me to a precipice. Jesus dumb, Jesus deaf, Jesus blind, heal me. How long is it since Ash and I watched the dawn horses gallop here, from field to field? Almost five years since our parting, since Ash became an impediment in my dreams just as surely as if in my speech. We came to a frontier, Ash and I, we paused; hesitated, parted, moving unsteadily at first until she began to run across those fields, obediently running. I did not attend her wedding, though I was invited. I long for her yet wish to cleanse my life of her influence. When we were both growing weaker, when Jake became determined to part us, it was she who first said, 'It's no good, Beth.' I had no answer. I remember there were small streaks of colour in the sky. Sunset. 'It's no good, Beth,' she said again and began to run. I watched her. She ran. Is she still running? I think it is a marathon, our race. It is not over yet. There are no winners.

FIVE

CARVED out of the turf that grows on the chalk uplands of this region, a giant 180 feet by 160 feet. The trenches of the giant's outline are cut a foot deep and a foot wide and the rain runs downhill and washes them clean and white. In his right arm he carries a club like that weapon Hercules carried, in his left what might be the hide of a slain lion. He stares bolt-eyed, his penis is huge, a white erection three thousand years old. Beth looks across the valley to observe the giant carved in the chalk of Giant Hill. A spring sunlight illuminates the giant's unanswerable fertility. Beth suspects that the giant knows she has been drifting aimlessly ever since Ash went away. Drifting, going wrong, yet expecting always to remain unhurt. Demanding to see her reflection preserved alive unchanging amid the landscape she and Ash once celebrated. Beth knows that she is drifting, that her thoughts stream indiscriminately beyond her grasp. She knows it and the giant confirms it. She stands on the summit of the hill and watches him.

He brandishes his club like the body of a newborn child. Beth stares at the white giant but will not let him suture her wounds. She remains trapped in the fever of her fidelity to Ash. She still moves via her backward zodiac, and dismisses the giant as a fetish-navigator, long out of fashion; and she turns downhill angrily, keeping her balance with difficulty on the slippery grass of the steep slope.

Restlessly she comes down into the ruins of the abbey and wanders among them. If she is searching, she finds nothing. Ash is not here. Ash has her own house, bright, noisy, modern, far away from these ruins. Does she still concern herself with thoughts of Beth? Or has she forgotten the summer they shared?

On this afternoon in the ruins, Beth swears like a blind woman approaching the source of her own decay. She walks in circles through the ruins until she is sickened by her repetitive journey and goes through the lych-gate into the churchyard. She threads her way between the old tombs, keeping her back to the giant. She is a female prisoner parading among the graves of lust and the rain falls on her, rank as Pharaoh's dream. She will not ask the giant to show her a way out of her trouble. 'Dear Ash,' she had written, 'I wonder if you ever remember our times together, fondly, or even mockingly . . . probably not, especially as you live so far away now. I am more likely to remember them, for I still live in the village . . .' Ash did not reply to the letter.

Beth shivers, the egg of the woman is like a lump of ice in her. She closes her eyes and sees Ash sewing, hemming black curtains. Like an ancestress, whispers Beth, just like that. Beth feels the rain going through and through her until she is no longer a woman but a rocky island. She shelters beneath a yew tree until the rain eases.

Ash paused on the stairs. She was five years older than Beth's memory of her.

I was never a holy woman! she thought resentfully.

Since the letter came, she had been thinking about Beth. She was worried because she knew Beth was not one to be strong against trouble. Her letter was full of hints of unhappiness. But I don't want to write to her or return to that . . . She heard the voices of her children upstairs. No, she decided angrily, no, I am not going to return, not even for a short visit, not to the village. It would spoil everything. I can still remember the way the twilight falls fingerless on the land there, misting me with fears, blurring me like an outrage. And how cold that Orion is, on the hill, in his white armour.

Ash shook her head and dismissed the thoughts that troubled her, thoughts of Beth, memories of their life together. She resumed her own life and climbed the stairs to her children, a bedtime storybook in her hand.

SIX

THERON was haunted. He was a sympathetic man by nature but he was haunted and the presence of the ghost stood between Theron and Beth.

The ghost was of his first wife. Vellet whispers to him, 'my dear Theron, I know our enemies are beginning their assault . . .'

And then that laugh of hers! Snaking along the corridors, her angry hiccup in his study. He flinches. Her shadow is always there. He is a sympathetic man but necessarily distant in his manner, because haunted, and less aware of Beth's unhappiness than he might otherwise have been.

And sometimes, mistaking Beth for her predecessor, he turns on Beth and speaks to her harshly. Beth is often immersed in her own thoughts and cannot defend herself. She has not seen the ghost yet.

Mostly Theron lets her alone, though. Weeks pass when husband and wife are strangers. Not enemies, but polite strangers, preoccupied with their own private emotions. Weeks pass without an embrace. Beth does not use contraceptives. It is part of her attitude of drifting, of her decision to be indecisive. She regards Theron's sexuality as neither important nor a threat to her. When he wants her, she will screw almost lazily with him and most times she comes but it doesn't mean very much to her. It means a brief forgetfulness of her troubles, but it does not change anything for her. Beth never considers that perhaps her feelings of isolation and panic might be caused by the poverty of their sexual life. She never makes the first approach to Theron. She does not ask herself why a young couple married less than two years should make love so infrequently. She is incapable of asking these questions, for she cannot look about herself with any clarity, she cannot consider the matter; it is only Ash, Ash, and the past . . .

And her husband is haunted.

SEVEN

THREE days before her death, Vellet and Theron argued violently. It began with a minor disagreement about the untidiness of the house. (Beth's tidiness was one of the qualities Theron valued, one he noticed particularly.) Vellet had hesitated for a moment but then turned on Theron, pointing at him, and shouting hysterically,

'I see your blasphemous books and I see your armies destroyed and once I thought I saw you slain by your own son. Remember, Theron, there are times when a slip of the tongue is high treason!'

'For god's sake,' yelled Theron, having heard all this before, 'just forget it, ok?'

But this response only infuriated Vellet and she shouted more shrilly,

'I carried my doorway under my arm, my heart made snarling noises but no one heard.'

She shoved him out of her way and ran out of the room.

It was on this occasion he became certain that he could not go on living with Vellet. They had friends coming to supper that evening, but all afternoon Vellet stayed in her room and refused to answer Theron when he attempted to persuade her to talk things over. They'd only been married two years at this time, and Vellet's always excitable temperament had in the last few months grown violent, morose and neurotic. Theron sat in his study that sour afternoon, his papers unread. He reflected that despite his academic qualifications as a military historian he could find no strategies to help in this situation. Vellet's sickness, as he had come to think of it, was a great sorrow, the greater since he had known Vellet from her childhood, from the time she and her father came to live in the village. Her father had died soon after the move, and as Theron was a distant (in fact the only) relation, a cousin several times removed, he became the old man's executor and guardian of Vellet. They had married immediately Vellet was legally of age.

The marriage caused talk in the village but Theron chose to disregard it. However, he acknowledged privately now that the gossips had been right, the marriage was a mistake. Vellet was too young, and he had exerted too much pressure on her, to persuade her into it.

He recalls her intent yet puzzled expression when they sat together in the summerhouse and he asked her to marry him. She had been reluctant, had caught her breath suddenly, in surprise or fear he could not tell.

He spoke to her persuasively though always in a straightforward and honest manner. To Vellet he seemed, as usual, withdrawn, grim in manner. And she had other more complex motives for not marrying him. He was an intruder, she felt. She sat beside him, gathering the green material of her dress into pleats, nervously moving in her mind between timidity and anger.

But all she said was that she had to think about her future before she could answer. He watched her walk away across the lawn, green and green. He watched her and began to gloat.

It was an evening some weeks later when she said yes, she would marry him. She accepted almost incoherently, unaware of real consequences. That afternoon she'd had a bad shock but she told Theron nothing about it. He had been over at the university all day and Vellet had gone secretively to meet a young unreliable friend. They had argued, the boy had come at her, grabbed her, wordblind, and she only just escaped from some violence, by ducking away, running out of the cottage, getting lost in the market crowds. When she got back home she locked all the doors and then decided, full of panic and foolishness, that she'd grasp the way out Theron offered her.

It was an evening with a grimy sky. The summer was going. The garden was shifting between white and black. After the words were said, all was set, planned, arranged, his touch and kiss no longer postponed, the shadows lapped around her, a dilapidation, and she was full of resentment.

Just before Christmas, on the day after her birthday, they were married, in the village church. The church was draughty, the parson disapproved of the whole business, the best man, a colleague from the university, had a bad cold and spoke his words hoarsely. That night Vellet told Theron she was nervous and so he went to his own room, touched by her ignorance. Vellet, in her room, the same room she'd occupied since she was a child, moved from bed to mirror to window to bed again almost blindly, fumbling and swearing. Her groin felt cold as ice. She went back to the window, stood there, trapped. How Vellet hated the thought of the life ahead of her, how, to her mind, she would be humbling herself every day.

She tried to avoid him, was very wary. He acknowledged her shyness and inexperience, but his patience did not last out the week. He had wanted Vellet since she was a schoolgirl. He had been patient a long time and he was sure it would work, this marriage, for his own emotions had been reflected upon Vellet for so long that he believed she was as intent upon their union as he himself. He went to her room. It was evening again, tense weather, not cold enough for winter. He paused, stood behind her, watching her in the mirror. She watched his reflection, without expression. Kindly, he asked her how she felt. She shrugged, then turned to him and tried to smile, yet she felt her body grow stiff, like a breakwater on a beach. He held her. For her this was exhausting, a punishment. There was a secret in her, old habits. She was unwilling to let Theron learn of or be responsible for those debts.

She searched arduously for an excuse but found none. When she was naked he touched her cautiously. The bed was like half the earth's surface, they were so separated on it, so much distance between them. When he touched the hair between her legs she found the sensation very unpleasant and could not hide her reaction from him. He thought it was her shyness.

The deep sound of pain that she uttered as he fucked her he mistook for a virgin's cry.

It was not.

The months went past until Theron sat in his study and thought of Vellet simply as a bringer of bad luck. That evening she came downstairs and prepared a meal for his guests. She enjoyed cooking. He watched her but she did not speak to him.

'You will speak sensibly to our guests?' he asked.

She looked at him and laughed sneeringly.

He turned away.

Four people, two men, two women sit around the table in a brightly lit room. Vellet has been silent so far. Theron has been talking nonstop to Bob and Lina but he cannot relax, feeling the radiation of Vellet's sullen discontent. His friends are shocked to see how bad things have become between Theron and Vellet and exchange sympathetic embarrassed glances.

Vellet broke her silence by saying that the dolphin is noted for the brilliance of its colours when dying. Theron poured out more wine, ignoring the remark.

'The meal was lovely, Vellet,' said Lina, smiling. Vellet sniffed.

'How are your silver mines in Joachimsthal, Bob?' she demanded, grimacing at him. He looked at Theron for guidance, but he only shrugged helplessly. Vellet laughed angrily. She poured the wine down her throat. She sat in her stiff petticoats, aching. She was sure that Bob and his woman were leering at her. The conversation turned to the presidential election, ignoring Vellet. She fingered the necklace that had been her mother's and wished she was outside in the dark, running through the winter darkness, climbing the hill to lie within the white boundaries of the giant and perhaps *he* would be waiting for her, the one she had wanted to escape, who had frightened her into this dead marriage, this abnormal event, she thought viciously. He cleared off when he knew the wedding was for real, went back to the city, left me here. If he hadn't threatened me . . . None of these people trust me. *He* did not trust me in the end and I got frightened of him, ran off, got into this mess. There are no more nights on the giant's back for me.

'Vellet?'

It is that woman with her dress decaying on her back. I stare at Lina.

'Are you coming to the concert next week, Vellet?' I lean forward across the table. Lina smells of pale mauve flowers.

'No.'

'Why not?' she asks.

I can't be bothered to answer. She opens her mouth as if to say something more but changes her mind. I saw her look at Theron, there was lust in her glance. My brain ached as I listened to the calm conversation around me. Then I stood up, I had to, and I danced around the room, I wanted them all to move, to dance, or to break, these solid bodies, I wanted us all to start screwing, wanted the night to keel over and for us all to copulate, I told them what I wanted, I told them, and their faces loomed towards me, simian and pale, cold, so calm, bloody calm. I wanted to dance, yes, and to fuck, to sing and shout, break out of this foreign territory. But all they did was to speak to me in warning voices. I saw how they looked knowingly from one to the other. Theron said something to Lina very quietly, I could not hear it. She took hold of me and tried to lead me out of the room. I was swaying and sobbing, and I felt sick, I shouted at her, your mouth is full of shit, but she was stronger than I was and she dragged me upstairs and I couldn't fight them any more, I lay across the bed as if I was paralyzed, and then when she thought I was asleep she went downstairs. I heard the murmur of voices in the hall as she and Bob left, hushed voices as if in a hospital or mad house. When Theron came and stood by my bedside I pretended to be asleep and after he'd gone I thought, all of this is killing me.

EIGHT

BETH said, 'supper's ready.'
Theron flinched.
'Must you interrupt me when I'm busy,' he asked bitterly, not looking at her.
'Didn't you hear me come in?'
'No,' said Theron, 'I was thinking.'
He was thinking of how Vellet got up from the bed and pulled the curtain back from the window and all they could see was night and she said, I cannot stroke night with my open hand, can you?
Beth stood beside her husband, watching him. Then she shivered, moved, knelt by the fire. For an instant she had seen a shadow leaping over his body.
He was thinking of how Vellet laughed at him and told him there was a lot he didn't know about her, she screeched at him and he slapped her across the face, but she went on laughing, and he thought he did not dare go on living with her any longer because he did not know what humpback secrets she was concealing. He had been afraid of her then. I am still afraid of her, he thought, unaware of Beth's gaze, of her possible compassion. She watches from the fireside. I am still afraid, he thought, Vellet is in the doorways, guardian of the doors. She is on the other side of all doors and she will not let me live in peace. She will transmute me from silver to a base metal. She will not stop haunting me.
'Shall we eat now,' asked Beth.
He scowled at her.
'Don't you know the dangers,' he muttered.
Red and silver fish swam along her veins. She shook her head. He pushed his chair back roughly and went out of the room, out of the house, doors banging. Beth did not know what violations she was guilty of. She remains on her knees by the fire. She wanted to thrust her hands into the flames but she did not dare. The pain she

endured was sharp, she wanted to replace it with a physical hurt, but she did not dare. I feel torn to pieces by this man who is always edging away from me. There in the flames I see a woman's face, not mine, nor the face of Ash. A stranger, a very young woman, very unhappy. Who is she? I begin to think that I must approach Theron more boldly, and learn what troubles him. I am frightened of doing this but I think we will both suffer a great deal more if we remain locked in our two solitudes. He is calm for long periods of time, calm, easygoing and then he behaves like this, so driven and inexplicably angry. Why? I must ask him straight out. I must have an answer. And I will tell him about my problem, my unresolved interest in Ash, which I don't know whether to call love or not. The days come and go with such vehemence and our questions must be answered.

Beth hears the wind and rain tearing through the rose-garden. She pictures her husband walking along the dark lanes between the fields, across the land salted with prehistoric bones.

She puts her hands against her cheeks scorched from the fire and says, I won't give another thought to Ash, or to the past.

In the room there is a woman's violent laughter. It is not Beth laughing. She jumps up, switches on the light. She is alone in the room. She looks all round the room, opens the door, goes out into the hall. The house is silent. Only the fire spits and crackles. Beth shrugs, settles to read the newspaper, to wait for Theron's return.

On Giant Hill in the dark, who is the woman dancing the egg dance? Who follows Theron when he walks in the woods where certain leaves throw forked shadows?

It is Vellet. She follows him. And sometimes on these night walks she fawns on him, whimpers, and the white of her drowned body is like the white of a bird's egg. She pleads for him to touch her and he must put out his hand, touch that chill breast, that chiller sex, before she will leave him.

Theron returned to the house, alone, disgusted, exhausted. In their bedroom south of Moscow he lectures his wife irascibly and she listens in silence, as if under an assumed name. She is sitting up in bed, an old crocheted shawl round her shoulders, and she notices how drawn his face is, how tired he looks. Suddenly he shouts, making her jump.

'Nobody must touch your watery shadow! Nobody! Nobody must finger your damp hair!'

Who is he talking to?

He bends over Beth and shouts in her face,

'Do you understand?'

He glares at her and the supperless girl brushes the night aside with her hands.

'I understand you,' she answers. She recalls their picnics on the beach, their walks in the snow, happy scenes, and she obliterates these memories with one inward dove cry. Then she turns out the light.

Theron fucked Beth but he was a receiver of stolen goods and he knew it. When he was asleep, Beth slipped out of bed and sat by the last of the fire. Her orgasm was useless for it was an experience unshared. It must be shared, she thought fiercely, letting her head loll between her hands, too tired to sleep. She was contained completely within the night now, dark and stale. She stared at her fingernails and smelt the stench of dead flowers in the room. She thought of knives, but only from a coward's point of view. If there was a place of safety, a protected place, she would go there and make Theron accompany her, no matter how many gangsters and ordeals stood between them and the sanctuary. But there is no safety, she reflected, only an endless series of cruel and grinding tasks in the day and at night orgasms so meaningless they become menacing. There's no bright world of acrobats and dancers, only the world of the wedding ring and the dark, prayers and semen, the night's events.

NINE

A COLD day in the late spring of 1972 with little weary patches of sun and the hollow roar of an east wind. Beth is walking through the village, greeting acquaintances, smiling, nodding, but she does not pause to converse. She walks on, climbing steadily up, until she is clear of the village and at the crossroads. She does not pause here, but turns and takes a familiar road.

On either side of the road, rough fields spread out. The light brown stony earth is also familiar to Beth. It is high ground here and the wind is colder. The sun deletes shadows far off into distances.

The house stands alone, at the edge of the moorland. It is uninhabited, no one wants to rent a house in such an isolated position, unmodernized and chilly.

Beth had been brought up in this house by her aunt. To keep the child company, her aunt had adopted a boy, Jake, a year younger than Beth. But this arrangement never took, the boy was never at home in the house or with the woman and the little girl. He'd been overseas in the army when Aunt Ann died. He'd joined up when he was sixteen, as a private soldier. Aunt Ann had regarded this as an act of defiance, for he could have waited until he was older, she said, and gone in with a commission. She never forgave him for enlisting, and left her house to Beth.

Beth went on living at the house on her own. There was just enough money left, carefully managed, for Beth to get by on, and she started her studies at the nearby university.

It was at this house, during the summer vacation that her friendship with Ash developed, a summer friendship that turned cold, left them both prey to shivery fits of sadness, the chill shadow of which reaches out to Beth now, at the gate, as she thinks back over the days before her marriage.

In all the windows of the house she sees reflections of that past summer, catalogues of happy evenings, walks with Ash, gardening, growing tomatoes in the greenhouse; and other reflections, of loss, misery.

Jake turned up at the house unexpectedly. He was out of uniform. It was in the evening, at the end of their summer. Beth and Ash met him on the back lawn, on the way home from their ride on the moor. He was looking up at the bedroom windows. When he turned to speak, Beth hardly recognized him, hadn't seen him for over two years. But her first thought was, he wants Ash.

The empty house stands in a tangle of old overgrown paths and marigold lawns now. The orchard has been swindled out of its picnics long ago. Beth pushes the gate open, walks around the side of the house, her feet scrunching on the gravel. She peers in through a window at sheeted furniture and quiet bare fireplaces. Across the lawn, beyond the greenhouse and the air-raid shelter, a dank pool lets the sky fall into its keycold waters. Beth stares down at the water, deep enough to drown in, and watches the wind ruffle the surface. She turns to look at the house again, at the sky reflected in the windows. Squarish, constructed of local grey stone, overlooked by no neighbours, the house keeps nothing hidden in its history. It is an ordinary house. No murders were committed in this house. No wizard rushed from room to room on the top floor, no planets sizzled from his finger-tips. No mad naked lady wild for elopement ever wrestled with her brothers and sisters on the stairs. No robbery, no fire, no plague. Even the air-raid shelter turned out to be unnecessary, despite the war-time air-base only ten miles across the moor. No bombs fell. No tragedies, only the commonplace events, natural death, ordinary arguments, moments of happiness, partings, the ending of friendship. Only the usual days and nights resembling sleep happened here. Marriage and birth, divorce and death, generations following the fossil-footprints downward.

Beth sits on an old bench by the pond and looks up at the far window, the room that was hers, when she lived here. Then her gaze moves across the brickwork and down until she stares at the back door. She is too far away to see the horse-shoe nailed on the door, but she knows it is there, pouring out good luck.

She closes her eyes. A few cold drops of rain are in the wind, the tough wild daffodils, small and pale, are entangled in the wind, there is a sudden spurt of moorhens across the water.

Beth opens her eyes. One autumn morning very early, mist sprouting everywhere, the back door was opened by a young woman in a long fur coat who hesitated in the doorway for a moment and then ran across the lawn, her thoughts like blood-birds, her feet protected only by thin slippers that were soon heavy with dew. The girl ran until she came to the pond. She stared down at the water, her hands clenched by her sides. Beth recognizes herself, no-one's daughter. On this autumn morning she is not yet married to Theron. The ceremony is to take place this afternoon. Beth watches the video of her memory. Her thin body is going back, she has almost become that memory, crawling into its skin. Her younger self paces the marshy edge of the pond. Between words and between gestures, thinks Beth, watching, I rediscover myself.

The autumn version of Beth looks back at the house, her face changes from one season to another, and Beth sees in that face the last of her own countrified virginity. The girl is gone back towards a future Beth has not yet understood. How often, she thinks, in that autumn and winter did I find myself standing by my bedroom window, our bedroom window, staring out at a frozen garden. I remember the frost, the snow, the life in a different house, how I felt marriage to be a sort of conscription. I did not care then where I was, or what my life meant, but now I require more than indifference, more than the chill that preserves but does not nourish.

She gets up from the bench. The clouds are blowing across the sky, she catches a glimpse of the blue lawlessness of the sky.

I feel I can swing free from the next winter if I can only recall one suitable word for the ice and ache of winter, if I can find a password to transform winter. I have nearly six months grace. My mouth will not be colder than winter this time. When I turn away from the window I will not go down into darkness. There have been too many of those days, when I have watched winter, frozen to my unreal bones. It must be different next winter.

She closes the garden gate, walks back to the crossroads. Beth wants something better than gardens of cold flowers.

Twilight was beginning when Beth reached the village. The streets were deserted. She could not say exactly what the visit to her old house had taught her, other than the warning against winter, but it seemed to her that the afternoon had given her some important knowledge that she must learn to translate. She walked along slowly, thinking over her experience, when she was suddenly surprised to hear Theron talking to someone. She looked around and saw in the dim light her husband and a young woman, a stranger to her, conversing at the end of a narrow passage leading to Church Street. Beth called out to him but he didn't seem to hear her. She began walking towards them but stopped short when she heard him say angrily,

'I see the shadow of lichen growing on your face . . .'

Struck by his strange words and the passion of his tone Beth paused and then drew aside into a doorway in the alley. She could not recognize the woman Theron addressed for she was in shadow. The woman laughed and said,

'The god of doors is blind, Theron, he cannot see my face.'

The woman's voice, cold and complacent, frightens Beth. She presses back against the damp brickwork, then peers forward, listening. The woman whose identity is hidden from Beth speaks again.

'Pretend sunday is my birthday, Theron. Will you celebrate with me? Will you laugh at my vaginal jokes?'

The woman's laughter echoes down the alleyway and hits Beth with the force of a reptile believed to be extinct. She shivers. Then she heard Theron say,

'Fires in my skull died down when Beth came to me.'

The woman swore then, viciously, obscenely about Beth, and Beth, shuddering, thought, I am walled up in the rain.

Theron said roughly,

'You offered me dry inedible fruit, how could I exist on that? Did you expect me to be content with that?'

Beth edged closer, trying to catch every word.

'I offered you freshly-killed hearts,' the woman told him tensely, 'I offered you the full moon penned in a glass bottle. I showed you how to march up to the Giant and get whatever you wanted.'

'No, no,' he said, 'you wore a dress of dragon bones and offered me the executioner's domain.'

It is as if the words choke Theron.

The woman said,

'I walk every night and see the moon disappear into the clouds of night. I see trees, ditches, rough grass. I am alone. I walk every night. Last night I came to the church and looked up at the belltower. An ugly old woman leaned out and cackled at me. Can you possibly imagine how cold my existence is, Theron?'

He answered,

'Liar, you liar, you always were. You could sleep amid bones and bodies forever. All that you complain of you brought on yourself.'

She drew her breath in sharply. Then she muttered,

'I foresee the death of your son. I foresee you lost amid fishes and flowers and firearms. All your wives are crazy. I know these things. I am certain of it all. I try to keep the records straight, Theron, even though I feel like a computer invaded by spiders.'

'Shut up, you bitch, shut up! I've had enough. I'm sick of conversations like crossword puzzles, I'm sick of you. Why don't you leave me alone, you know I won't give you anything.'

The woman moved a little away from Theron and to Beth it seemed that she was considering him sadly, and she spoke quietly,

'If my words are distorted, it is by a virus I can't be cured of. You have isolated me. You know the place I inhabit and you chose it for me, Thêron. Can you blame me for clinging to you, Theron. You are my only link with the old ways. I cannot help it if I can only meet you in these dark places. I do not choose the time or the place for my . . . manifestations. I want to speak clearly, to speak and live the truth. But I am silted up for good, with no hope. The first and strongest emotion I experience is anger: it is my major key. I see anger in the snow-geese of winter, in the headlands, the sea, in all the duties of this existence of mine that is no existence. I taste anger in birdseed, I hear it in the songs of birds. All the rooms I inhabit are warped. All my memories are waterlogged. I am unable to make sense of my aloneness. I'm still on the brink of the river, at the brink of my death.'

Then there was a silence like an archaeological investigation of the blood of the man and the two women. It was now quite dark and the rain was falling steadily, promising sleeplessness.

Beth crept closer until she was near enough to reach out and touch Theron's shoulder. She shivered, drenched with the rain.

She crept closer until she saw the lichen shadow on the other woman's face, her skin stained with waterweed.

'Who are you?' Beth cried out, in terror.

Theron swung round and stared at Beth.

'There's no one here, no one,' he gabbled, 'come away, there's no one here . . .'

But Beth saw the woman and pushed Theron aside, with the strength of her terror, and he fell against the wall, he groaned. The woman began to back away, very slowly, her pale eyes fixed on Beth, her smile decaying in the rainy shadows, retreating into the street beyond the alley. Beth followed her and asked her quietly,

'Who are you?'

The answer came in a voice of no simplicity.

'Vellet. Vellet.'

And the echo went down the alley, into the darkness which it charred.

TEN

IT IS morning and Beth and Theron are eating bacon sandwiches for breakfast. It is very early, an iron-hard light with no sun. Outside, the wind slews round. Beth gets up from the table, leans on the windowsill and stares out at the rainy day that is coiled like a snake about them both.

Last night he refused to answer any of Beth's questions. He did not get angry. He did not respond in any way. He was armoured against each attack. She wept, she screamed, she coaxed, she threatened. He would not answer one single question.

'Why did she call herself by your first wife's name? Who is she? What is wrong with her face? Do you sleep with her?'

He shook his head.

'Who is she?'

'Don't ask me these questions, Beth, please,' was all he said, over and over again.

Now he drinks his coffee, looks understandingly at Beth, asks her to rest today, says no more, except that he'll be home at the usual time. Then he leaves the house.

Fifteen minutes later Beth is thinking, no, not blood, not blood-stains today, please, no blood when I wipe myself.

But there is blood. The blood flows from Beth's womb. Her back aches, pain presses her breasts in its cramping bodice. She pauses as she is about to switch on the washing-machine and thinks, what kind of man have I become wife to?

Last night he had caught Beth and stopped her from running after the other woman and getting any information from her. By the time she had struggled free, the street was empty, the woman (was there a woman?) had gone.

Now Beth is without any plans or ideas about her own future. Can I possibly expect a good end from such bad beginnings? Beth shakes her head.

Later that day she went to sit in the little back sitting-room that looked out on her favourite part of the garden, where the roses grew. She sat by the window, an old cardigan thrown over her shoulders. On her lap is a book and she is studying a picture of the Creator carrying the sleeping Adam. She concentrates on this, memorizing every detail, for ten minutes, until a sudden whining gust of wind makes her jump. The window sashes rattle. The book slips to the floor. She makes a movement as if to pick it up but changes her mind, scratches her arm, stands up, stretches, yawns. She buttons the cardigan on and peers out of the window at a dull afternoon, a conversation in another language. Taking a couple of tissues out of her pocket, she wedges them into the window frame, to stop the rattling. She kneels on the windowsill and glares out at the fuzzy sky, the few stealthy birds, as if her angry stare might alter the weather. She remembers the colour of rainwater that collects in the hoofprints the cattle leave on the hillside of the Giant: it is the colour of her thoughts. She thinks of the other house, beyond the village, high up on the moors, and wishes she were there.

The half-touch of cramp still lingers but the blood has settled to an even flow and only her slight pallor might hint at Beth's menstruation. She breathes on the window and on the misted glass writes with her forefinger, Ash . . .

But she is thinking of Theron, and the mystery woman. What does his silence mean? Is he afraid? Of me? No, more likely of her. How did she manage to vanish so quickly? I heard no car drive away. What is between Theron and this woman who has appropriated his first wife's name?

Beth sets her lips, determined to show her contempt for the threats of this woman. She does not know that Vellet has cursed Theron, put an attacking army in his mind.

She rubs out the name on the window and quickly gets her coat, goes outdoors, uneasy with desires she only half acknowledges, disturbed by the strength of her concern for Theron. She'd married him in a careless way, liking him, admiring him, but also detached from any deep sustaining relation with him, she had wished only to blot out all memories of Ash and of the house on the moors where she and Ash had been happy for a while. It was an offhand beginning, straight out of the pain of losing Ash, and Beth is disturbed now to find how deeply she cares about her marriage and fears for Theron's safety.

Up to now their life has worked, drifting, not going deep, but bringing something into their lives, mutual support and shared interests. Beth moves slowly across the garden, through the snarled passages of rain. Now that Theron is intimidated by a stranger and has become more remote and troubled, Beth feels all her emotions roused. She knows she must learn what is isolating him. She does not know that whenever she walks towards Theron, he sees a ghost over her shoulder.

She heads out of the garden, away from the village where her enemies are too strong for her as yet, and walks up through the woods, through Rowden Foot Coppice, until she comes to Giant Hill. At the foot of the Hill, beside the little spring into which she often throws a coin, but not today, she meets the old tramp the villagers call Funeral Jo. He grins at her. He was sitting on a tree trunk, wearing an old grey plastic rain coat, a torn pair of corduroy trousers and layers of newspaper. 'Hello, Jo,' said Beth, 'when's summer going to begin?' He just shook his head wisely. Smiling, Beth walked on through the abbey ruins and began climbing the hill. As she went up through air cold as interrogations she thought, it is not the sky that this giant supports on his shoulders, but the land and all of us on it, all our blindness and recklessness. The grass is slippery and Beth has to go carefully. Another woman watches Beth struggle up the hill but Beth does not see her. The woman who watches from a never-to-be-discovered hiding place whispers, go to the snout of the dungeon, Beth. Beth does not hear these words. The woman with the skin of a hunter sits in her cold forest.

At the summit of the hill, Beth looks along the white expanse of the Giant, the archaic form. Lost in thought, Beth stands for some minutes without moving a muscle, then breaks away, as if out of a spell, looks down to see the long distance of flowing water, the river that skirts the foot of the hill. But she looks again at the giant and moves to meet him, fearfully, with the indistinct vowel sounds of supplication rising to her lips.

She sits or rather squats down between the eyes of the giant. It is not fitting for her to sit on his breast or on his penis. The white yards of him stretch about and around her. She crouches on the cold grass. Her blood flows. The landscape is grey mostly, like a bad smudgy drawing, and the rain has become fine and constant.

Beth offers the giant her loneliness that is like the biting of some animal.

All my life, she thinks, I have believed in the giant. Perhaps I am the first person for many years to love the giant. I am the first enemy of any darkness that hates him. Local people either ignore this huge figure cut into the chalk thousands of years ago, this marcher, this fertile sign, or, if there is any reaction, it will be an embarassed snigger, a gesture of obscenity. Though perhaps I am being unfair, too hasty. I believe that there may be some, women, perhaps, or young men, who turn towards the giant, seriously, considering his advice. I have tried to keep faith. When I was in my teens, I would cycle over here in the school holidays or at weekends, and read, or think, or dream. He is a focus for dreams, here the energies of dream come into the everyday life, bringing incisiveness, strength, beauty. Or so it was for me. And there is a peacefulness here that I never found in a church. And always behind the peace is energy, which gives me life, and yet which some people, Ash, yes, and Theron, say they find too much to cope with, too alien a sensation, an electric shock, that causes them to have nothing to do with the giant. In the summer, coaches come and strangers on day-trips clamber up Giant Hill, and I've seen them flinch behind their cameras from the prehistoric man, dancer and warrior.

Seated between his eyes, below the summit of the hill, Beth is sheltered from the wind but the rain drives at her. She touches the chalk of his left eyesocket with her left hand, and speaks to the giant.

I remember an autumn years ago when Ash and I sat here. It was sunny but getting on for evening. Ash still had long hair then and as she told me a strange story she plaited and unplaited the ends of her braids. I remember watching her face, the expressions changing, sadness, sustained courage, shame, anger.

This was her story.

When I was sixteen (said Ash) I left home and got a job as a waitress in a cafe in the poorer district of the city. I had lived in the city all my life and the ugliness of it had had years to get right behind my eyes: crowds, noise, traffic, the silent howl of the living, the violence at the edge of everything. At night, Beth, at night when I slept I did not dare dream. I went from day to day without looking backward or forward, an automaton. I did not dare enter any church in the city although I needed rest and sanctuary. I did not read any newspapers because disasters frightened me, drew me in to their dark to erase me. Obliteration was everywhere. I felt my own blood pour out on the pavement of the city which sheltered so many terrorists. Bomb-blasts deafened me. I worked in that filthy caff, numb and frightened, for nearly two years. One winter morning, the rain pouring down, a tall well-dressed man with a loud hoarse voice came into the stuffy room and glanced at me without smiling.

(Ash paused, took a deep breath, glanced around her at the fields, at her friend listening intently, and resumed.)

For no apparent reason, I was afraid. Even more afraid than usual! I looked away and deliberately took another customer's order. I saw the tall man talking to the manager and at one point in their conversation, I saw both men look over at me coldly. That evening I packed my belongings in a single cheap suitcase and left my room in the boarding house. Carrying one book in my gloved hand I went to the address the manager had given me.

The tall man, whose name does not matter, opened the door. He took my suitcase and smiled formally. There was something motionless about him, a stillness beneath his skin. Who are you? I asked roughly. He offered me a drink. I shook my head. I am not one who guides people through the dark, he said. I did not understand him and I said so. It does not matter, he answered. The room was very cold, I shivered. He switched on an electric fire. Then he stood by the window and looked at me intently, although the room was dark and my face lit only by the fake logs of the fire. Listen, he said quietly. I nodded. He spoke for sometime without looking at me. When he'd finished, he asked, do you understand? Yes, I said. Don't tell lies, he said sharply.

(Beth started to ask Ash a question, but Ash motioned her to be quiet. She went on speaking very rapidly now, to get the pictures out of her head.)

Very well, I said to the man, I don't understand. He was silent. He tapped on the window with his forefinger. It will be a comfortable life for you, he said, softly. You will not have to work all day and half the night in a miserable fish restaurant. This existence of yours in the city will become . . . extinct, as it were. I live a long way from here. You will find difficulties at first, it will be strange, but you will settle down. Do you follow me now? I said, I think so. I thought, Beth, of fool's gold and of the Chevalier Raoul. My head throbbed, I felt feverish. He came towards me and looked at me. I could tell now that he was still young, in his thirties, but tired. You are poor, he said, and, I suspect, desperate. Do you accept my offer? I said nothing. He frowned, then sighed. The dark room stirred with rape and horror. I knew that came from *outside*, from the city, not from him. I looked out of the window at those streets and alleyways and I shuddered. Yes, I said, yes, I agree, in a voice I hardly recognized as mine. Yes. Yes. Good, he said casually. We'll set off first thing in the morning.

He showed me to a small bedroom and here I passed the night alone, without sleeping. In the morning we left the city by car. It was still raining heavily. I was so happy to be leaving. I glanced at the man. I saw no hump on his back. I thought of my hands, Beth, full of money! We drove all day and in the early evening stopped at a modest hotel. Again we had separate rooms. The idea of his sex scared me, yet fascinated me. I had this persistent idea in my mind, I must have read it somewhere, that the empty silken garments of a lover can be abandoned to bring fair weather. As we ate breakfast, he asked me if I was pleased with the new arrangement. In my life, I supposed. I said I did not know. After breakfast, while I was packing, he came into my room and locked the door. He talked to me for nearly an hour. Then we set off again. The rain had lifted and I looked out of the car window curiously at green hills and fields. I was excited. Think, Beth, the city girl's outing. This journey took place in the second month of the year. Yes, I was excited, but I felt tense, little daggers touched my breast.

We arrived at our destination in the afternoon. It was a big house with well-kept grounds. When I walked into the house, my clothes felt dirty on my skin. A woman, older than the man, came slowly downstairs to meet us. She looked ironically at us. You see, said the man, I have been successful. He gestured lightly towards me. Have you? she said coolly. So my life in that house began.

That night I gathered the threads of the life together. He came to my room but did not touch me. He took off his clothes and put on the clothes of a woman. He looked at himself in the mirror for quite a time and then asked me to dance with him. It was a formal dance, without music. As we danced he said to me, my sister won't do it, and my wife's dead, so you see I need you. I stroked the folds of his dress, as he suggested. I vowed to avoid anger, lust, cowardice, malevolence in this new life.

I was introduced to visitors as his secretary, but I suppose a good many of them guessed I performed another function. At first I managed, the man was kind, demanded, you see, almost nothing. The sister hated me, what else could you expect. I stayed there for nearly a year, a lazy life, really, with plenty of freedom, money, better than working in the caff, away from the city. But then contempt built up in me, for him and for myself, and I found unexpected strength in myself, enabling me to break away from that corrupt association. No angry event precipitated my leaving, all happened in a civilized manner, and we parted friends.

Beth is shivering in the rain. Another of Ash's histories. Another of her anecdotes. Beth knows them by heart.

She makes her way home.

On her table there is an open bible and a glass vase with a bunch of lilies blue as the mountains of Jephthah's daughter.

When Beth came in her feet felt bruised as if she'd been walking barefoot and her head ached. She went straight to the living-room and lit the fire she'd laid this morning, kneeling down to witness the sacrifice of summer trees. Little flames soon glide through the twigs and the odour of woodsmoke appeases Beth. An alphabet of unhappiness burns away in the fire, relieving Beth's tension for a while. A fire for the giant, she whispers. There is silence except for the fire and Beth sees pictures in the flames. She sees stars, the ships of the left hand, a woman with honeymoon claws, a child dressed in membraneous clothes, sneakthief faces, the serene smile of the hobgoblin.

Beth jerks her head up. She was almost asleep. She moves back from the heat of the fire, sits in the comfortable old colonial chair she'd brought from her own house. She felt a strange indiscriminate peace now, the calm of the last day of a saturnalia. It is because of my period, thought Beth, and it will not last. The arrears remain. But I will accept it while it lasts, without bribery, threats or promises.

And still Ash is behind all Beth's thoughts, numinous, like a sun or a star.

But did I ever, thinks Beth, really believe any of the accounts of herself Ash gave me? Surely I always knew they were her fantasies? Not lies, no, but elaborations of smaller far less exciting adventures. When I think of it, I know nothing at all about her life before she arrived at the village, out of nowhere.

Ash, you were walking along Half Moon Street and I almost bumped into you as I came out of the grocer's. Where are you going, I wondered, at once drawn to you, inexplicably then, but now I believe it was because at that time you and I were so similar that we made the perfect reflection, one to the other. It was late in the afternoon, and the shadows would have hidden me, but I did not dare follow you. Your face was, without doubt, one I was unable to read, and yet felt compelled to consider. The reflection, you see.

Now, years later, I am possessed by the desire to know whether we are still the same reflection, split into two halves, or whether we have grown to be different. I want to know, I suppose, whether we have grown up. I am listening to the past, as to a wound, and I need to change that habit. Blood's given language could map our hearts, if we met now. The masks of twilight crowd around me, whispering, Ash, Ash.

And drowning out that sound is the engine of Theron's car revving up and then stopping outside the door.

ELEVEN

A FORTNIGHT after the encounter in Church Street, Theron and I walked over the fields to the river. It was late on Sunday afternoon. I could sight-read the trees, I saw the summer coming towards me, its glossy green candles and its white anointments. But when Theron glanced at me, I saw the sky become dank and graceless rain threaten. His voice was cold and calm. He spoke of an article he'd read in the morning's paper. He tells me that in his opinion abortions are illegal operations. I felt no need to reply.

We walked along the towpath in silence until we came to the bench donated by a former mayor of the village where we sat down. A little further upstream two boys were rowing in an old dinghy but no other vessels were on the water.

I looked at Theron. He has been sleeping badly and he holds his body in a rigid way, as if avoiding some disgrace. I am afraid he is becoming ill. I do not think he has seen the woman again but he will not speak of that night at all. We've only made love twice since then. I have stopped asking questions. He ignored everything I said. I have just the words of one language at my disposal and my dialect can only cope with so many riddles at any one time. So I've stopped asking questions.

Beth puts her hand gently on Theron's shoulder. The sunlight glitters on the brown water of the river. The little boys row to the opposite bank and are calling to their friends, who help pull the boat in to shore. Theron's smile is forced, cold as the shadow of a dog. Beth sees how his unhappiness encumbers him. Specks of blood are falling on the page of a book of jokes.

'Lets walk on, shall we? To Giant Hill?' She spoke softly. He nodded and for an instant Beth smelt the body of his first wife rotting in the orchard, but she pushed this image away with the damp groping hands of a timid child. Oh this man is to blame! she thought savagely, irrationally, knowing she was being unfair.

Theron opens the wooden gate at the end of the towpath and they walk along a street of settled houses surrounded by bright flowers and quiet cultivated lawns. Theron's remark startles her, the more so in these domesticated surroundings.

'Beth, your hair whispers like her . . .' She turns sharply on him.

'What? My hair? Like hers? Whose?' She tugged at his sleeve, bringing her face close to his.

'Whose, Theron?'

He shrugged, was suddenly petulant.

'Forget it, it's nothing. Just a dream I had, last night. A fragment, remembered. Just came into my head. I was thinking aloud, that's all.' Beth relaxes and slips her hand into his. This is the first real confidence he's made for weeks, the first real contact.

'Tell me, please.'

Theron walks on rapidly, pulling her with him. The windows of the new houses are stone deaf but not blind; Theron and Beth flash in each window they pass like a newsreel.

'In my dream,' he said, 'it is twilight in a moon city, and the wives of senators are decked out in their pearls. I am one, I think, but I have no wife. I drink but the wine makes me weep. My mother comes into the room and a veil is clinging to her hair and makes me think of spidery crabs crawling there. She twitches the veil off and says to me, blood keeps me clean, son. I shout at her, red flowers, mother, red flowers I accept, but no blood. And that was my dream.'

Beth and Theron turn out of the street and enter a leafy shadowy lane.

'No, wait. There was more. I remember now. In the dream mother says, you act the fool but I know that you are clever enough when you choose to be. Her voice is very soft, Beth, and it is like hair moving in the breeze. She says to me, I will walk another mile and then I will rest. I am collecting Vellet's excrement.'

Theron gasps out the last sentences as if rebelling against them but unable to help himself. Sweat stands out on his face. Beth does not know what to say, hesitates. Theron takes a shuddering breath. They are at the foot of Giant Hill. The sun is moving restlessly among clouds and the air is growing colder. Theron remembers his dream with bitterness.

'You know who Vellet is?' he asks Beth.
'Yes. Your first wife.'
He nods, can't speak, lights a cigarette.
'It is perhaps natural to dream of your first wife,' she suggests, frowning anxiously.
'It was so repellent in the dream, Beth.' He is calmer now, draws on the cigarette. They pause by the stile, do not climb over.
'There must be a meaning in a dream, always, so I've read,' says Theron, 'but what is in this dream?'
'It is hard to read dreams, Theron, hard to lift them out of their dark, and no one meaning will ever be found, only the variables, which must serve.' Beth spoke with profound tenderness, leaning towards Theron. 'Can you recall any more of the dream, my dear?'
He concentrated, fixing his gaze on the ground.
'Yes,' he said slowly, 'yes. I see my mother holding excrement in her gloved hands and smiling at me. She offers it to me. Eventually I take it. It feels cold and dry. My mother goes away. But Vellet comes into the room, brushes her hair in front of the mirror. She says to me, *something swollen, Theron? Heart?* I have no answer. She goes out of the room, looking back over her shoulder, contemptuously. That is the end of the dream. What can it mean, Beth?'
When Theron looked at her with such unfamiliar intensity, such new dependence, fear like a sniper behind his eyes, Beth did not know what to say. She knew that if she found the right answer, the true answer, their lives would be changed and be immeasurably strengthened. But his dream had depressed her and she could think of no positive meaning in the dream, it seemed to her only another sign that Theron was very disturbed and that his dream was a symptom of some illness. She did not even want to think about the role his first wife Vellet still played in his life and this factor inhibits her sympathy. She does not know how to answer him without hurting him. Perhaps I should hurt him, she thought.
'Beth?'
She looked up.
'I think . . . I think it means there is some unresolved and unsuspected grief in you still, Theron, about Vellet. Some guilt? But why feel responsible for her death? Do you? It was accidental, her death.'

He struggled away from her embrace, uttering a long incoherent rambling string of words, a lawless bellow, anger choking him.

'Then consult a doctor,' she shouted after him, but he did not answer, he went on down the lane, leaving her by the stile, frightened and resentful. It was his bloody dream, she thought. She wanted at that moment to pack up her things and return to her house, on the high ground above the village. I can't help him. There are no clues. Unless the dream is a clue. But how complex to unravel. I sense Theron is travelling new and difficult distances within himself. These take him not just away from me, but from all who might help him. That dream frightened me. He has become so changed lately. If I am to help him, he must give me all the facts. All the information, not keeping anything back. If it were a lecture, he would give all the facts to his students. He must do the same in this situation we're in. All the facts. How can I advise him otherwise?

She sat on the stile as the summer twilight came on. A remnant of travellers stumbled down through the trees and as they climbed the stile greeted her. She smiled and watched the two couples disappear around the bend in the path.

The idea of a summer spent alone at her own house fills her with pleasure but she will not go unless their troubles grow worse. I will not be driven out of this marriage until I learn more of Vellet. That is the heart of the trouble. It lies in the past. I'll ask in the village about his first wife. I'll ask Tabitha. She'll know.

Beth sits for a long while in the musky evening, thinking half against her will about Theron's dream, about his mother, the red flowers, the blood, Vellet, and her excrement, her contempt. When she walks home, the branches of the trees are like the strong tendons in the necks of animals. The moon is sewn to the church steeple.

But I am not ready, thinks Beth, to enter whatever labyrinth Theron and Vellet spun around themselves. I am not ready, but how can I avoid it. Something swollen? Heart?

When she got home, he'd made the supper and nothing was said of any dream or argument. He came to her room to say goodnight, last thing. He sat on the edge of her bed and apologized for his outburst.

'I was all on edge.'

Beth smiled.

'Why did that dream upset you so much, Theron. We all get these weird dreams.'

He shrugged, moved away from the bed.

'Overwork, I guess,' he said.

'Tell me about Vellet,' said Beth placidly, pulling her shawl around her shoulders. She was sitting up in bed, she'd been reading when he came in. He deliberately adopted an expression that was both stupid and solemn.

'It was a tragedy,' he said, 'we were very happy and then there was the accident. There's nothing to tell. She was very young. She was headstrong. She insisted on going for a swim though I tried to persuade her against it . . . I did not know she'd slipped out of the house that night, I thought she'd taken my advice. It is when I get overtired, then I dream of her. And dreams, you know, they are only distortions of our daytime thoughts, a sort of re-run, only jumbled and rotten.'

'Are they?' asked Beth.

'I brought you a book to read,' he said, placing it on her bedside table.

'Thank you, dear.'

He stooped and kissed her goodnight. He was aware of the sinews and ovaries of her body warding him off, she knew that.

He closed the door behind him. She picked up his book. A detective story. She throws it on the floor. I want none of his propagandas, she thinks, I want the truth. How neatly his mask fits! But it will suffocate him.

After he'd said goodnight to Beth, he tried to settle to some work, and went into his study. He drew the curtains, sat at his desk. As soon as he sat down, he remembered the night it began.

On that first night he could not sleep, so he got up and wandered out into the garden. It was a hot airless night. He was a widower, recently bereaved. Vellet had been buried barely a month.

He sat in the summerhouse and did not notice how the July air got strangely colder. But when he stood up to go indoors he saw her.

Oh god in the dark I saw her, a woman without shoes on her feet, without any garments.

She said, 'I am the water's woman, you cannot bring me back to life.'

I looked at her face and my darkness lifted.

I saw her sensuous shadow, her lap of luxury.

I did not know then her way of destroying, by inches.

She called me, 'Theron.'

She said, 'you know my name.'

I said, 'you have no name.'

But I was fascinated.

Aproned with storms, she came towards me.

I put myself into her hands.

So she trapped me. So began my haunting. So began the resurrection of Vellet.

Theron left his room. It was almost impossible for him to move but he lifted one foot and set it down again in a new position, carefully shifting his body in the direction of this new position, and so again with the other foot, and so on, until he managed to walk. He got to the kitchen and made himself a cup of chocolate, sat drinking it, still puzzling over the dream.

It never occurs to him that he might enjoy being haunted. It never occurs to him that he could exorcise Vellet, if he were to put his heart into it. To tell Beth about Vellet, that's unthinkable. So the haunting goes on.

TWELVE

IN a medieval cathedral in a European city, Ash looks up at a stained glass window representing the biblical girl Tamar.

Beth trudges across muddy fields near the village of the giant.

Ash steps up into the pulpit and reads silently from the huge open bible: 'Eat your flesh as fire.'

The rain slackens but Beth strides on. The man is cold, she rages, the man is cold.

Ash smiles slightly, flicks through the heavy pages of the bible. '. . . all the curses that are written in this book shall lie upon him . . .'

Ash's gaze returns to the stained glass window. Her Madonna wanders slowly through the snow. Her Christ's kisses darken her heart, as if Ash were exposed to wind and weather. She turns another page. '. . . the captive exile hasteneth to be loosed . . .'

In the black morning Beth hears white bells toll. She grips the field gate with her wet hands and imagines spiders pierced with golden needles. It is Theron who tortures them, she mutters. I want to face those sort of dangers without flinching. I know I am the life my fingertips fear. His unkind words this morning are none of my concern. Fuck him. I have to think of the anticipations of Eve, I have to quench my own thirst.

'. . . I have set her blood on the top of a rock . . .' Ash closes the book. She descends from the pulpit, she does not dip her fingers in the stoop of holy water. She goes out of the cathedral barn back into the city. She was weary. Yes, woman comes to it, approaching the edge, followed by the thieving birds of her shadow. She is intricate as lace-making, struck dumb by the risks she takes.

Meanwhile, Beth travels on to a bleak place, much feared by strangers. Yes, the man is cold, she thinks, but her rage has stilled. She has been crying and hitting out at her thoughts with her fists.

Now there is a sensation of steady driving warmth throughout her body and she takes shelter in an abandoned farm building within sight of Giant Hill.

The image of a red shroud flaps in my mind, as in a wind ripping down from the hill. This morning Theron and I discussed that dream and we argued again. We concentrated on his problems but mine were tucked well out of sight. I ask him about that woman but he refuses to answer. If we argue in the middle of summer, we are bound to argue next winter, when conditions are more generally unfavourable. When I have so little knowledge of my own self, how can I give him back the mystery of his dream, solved and safe for him to contemplate? I said to him, the dream is the message of the instincts, what it foretells will happen of itself, you do not have to do anything but allow the process to continue. When I told him this, which was the best I could do, he answered coarsely, you smooth stupid cunt, how would you know? He was pallid and his lips were puffy, like those of a premenstrual woman. There we stood, this morning, in the kitchen, surrounded by the shadows of pre-Christian men and unbaptized infants. On a threshold. Both of us at the border of a route that leads either to an orchard of lemon trees, paradisal, or to a cage of ooze, the slime and algae of our end.

But she will not leave Theron. She has the strength to cope with events of this morning's nature. There is much strength in Beth and she is beginning to understand this. Beth lives in a place where Vellet cannot go. She cannot slither into Beth's life. Vellet is afraid of this woman who has found calm, who can sit and think at the end of her rage, who has a delicacy of intellect that Vellet never possessed.

Vellet is watching Beth, from the other side of the rain. Then she turns to the Giant, her companion.

'Blindman, who am I?' she cries out. 'Who is this woman? How can she be so strong? Beth? Is this Beth? Giant, who is she?'

No answer for Vellet. Silence in the region of the Giant, that handicaps Vellet. I hate the woman, she thinks, and yet she cannot get close enough to Beth to communicate her hatred. There is a barrier preventing Vellet from contaminating Beth with her blue face and red rump, her bird's beak and her drowned hair.

'You look angry, Giant. You look angry all the time, to me. Is it because Beth's child will die one hundred years from now? Why were you blinded, Giant? Did you see stars that were forbidden, a moon with a woman's face? Why was I drowned? Why am I kept in this limbo, half-flesh, half-ghost? I had made up my mind to haunt Beth but she cannot, will not see me. What force is she exuding, that puts me in so close a paddock, eh, Giant? Are you giving her a helping hand? Help me too. Take these handcuffs of water off my wrists, Giant. Give me back my body, my breath. I won't get into unintelligible regions next time, I promise. Give me a new life. Let me go back and begin again.'

'There is a way to the next stage for you, Vellet,' the giant answered, in a delving voice, 'but you must find the door before you pick the lock. You are not ready for any new life yet. You still retard yourself.'

'Fuck!' said Vellet defiantly. And then, after a moment, sadly, 'who else will rescue me?'

'You have not asked the right question yet. Ask that question and you will be rescued.'

The two shadows, the two shades, converse between weathers, between fluctuations in the air, spirits of the place, perhaps, or the imagination of the hill searching for an utterance.

'I'm tired of all this talk, I didn't ask to be put here, stuck here with you, why should I stay here? There's no pleasure in it. Do you remember, Giant, years ago, when that boy and I came here at night to make love on the slopes of your hill? That was not Theron, but the other one, who I loved, but who frightened me, so that I ran off to marry Theron, and so lost him. We lay down on your slope and exchanged our greetings. There was a little moon that misled me and I let him do it. Did you feel it, Giant? Do you join in?'

Vellet paused, looked mischievous, but there was no answer from her companion.

'Anyway, it was the first time, for me. It was like walking on tiptoe down a steep valley towards a garden. Then he thrust into me, a man groping for a door in the dark. I knew he was thinking of another girl's face but I was too excited to care, I heard my body's havoc and I felt the world revolve wetly in the orifices of my body. I did not come but afterwards I realized I had been able for the first time to look deeply into the downpour of myself. Then he and I sprawled out on your hill, like victims of a bombardment. I trembled violently. If I had known my future, which death would I have chosen? Death by air? By fire? By water? Or by burial in the earth? But I knew nothing of my future. Is this story ammunition for your magic lantern world, Giant? No. You are hard as the earth you are carved from. I am a lost woman in a desert begging you for charity and you will not help!'

'I cannot help you. You must solve the riddle yourself.' The giant is falling back into the uncomprehending earth.

Vellet laughed unpleasantly. She climbed into the boughs of an elder tree and sat among the white flowers and black fruit.

'I suppose I am too wicked to be helped?'

'No. But it is not my business to help.'

'What is your business, Giant?'

'To remember the thinness of my own self. To understand my blindness.' This is the voice of the earth itself now and turning to dust. Vellet does not understand and dances across a red planet and back again to the edge of the giant. She rattles her anger in her throat. In her mouth, she always tastes the necromancy of a great salt lake.

'But I would eat my children as soon as I caught them,' she said, removing her gloves and taking the coins from her eyelids. She will not look at Beth, climbing the stairs to her bedroom. Vellet bleeds from breasts, hands and knees.

'Did you hear me, Giant? Eat my children!' The Giant laughed.

'You are clever at twisting words, Vellet.' Vellet laughed with him, for he was her puppeteer, her manipulator. He said sharply, 'Don't laugh.'

'I am the princess caught under the spell of an evil sorcerer,' she said. But she did not laugh.

Beth wielded the sharp knife expertly and sliced the raw meat. Theron watched her exact movements eagerly, but in silence, admiring her neat interlocking gestures as she prepared the meal. Suddenly he felt the alienness of himself return, felt a buffoon there in the kitchen, doing nothing.

'I'll go for a walk, the sun's coming out.' Beth nodded, absorbed in her task. Theron felt himself turning unavoidably into many shapes, none of them were what he wanted. He waved goodbye through the window. Beth waved back, her fingers bloody. Theron's own fingertips sighed on the black gate. Recently, he had read about the dwarf who mourned the death of his friend, a blind giant.

She sank beneath the water, he thought. And now paths of hawthorn and spittle mislead me.

The words of a man planning rebellion are always confused.

As Theron came down through the trees of Morning Well Plantation, he saw her by the gate, waiting for him. The sun encourages Theron to smile, but he does not notice the sunlight now. He is tired and his face looks worn.

She has followed me again, he thought dully. I have been walking along Vellet's corridor, that territory passing through a land to which it does not belong.

She put her hand out and touched his chest and said in a whisper, 'I saw you, Theron, naked and berserk, sweating with gaol fever. Why did you throw my photograph, torn to shreds, down the privy?'

He does not answer, begins to walk away. She follows him.

'You see, you have two wives,' she explains, smiling.

He opens the gate, walks rapidly along the path. A little stream glitters and winds beside the path. Vellet jumps and lands on the water, she is walking on the water. Theron watches this trick out of the corner of his eye disdainfully. Vellet careers over the water, stares down to see her own apparition heavy on the stream. In the field, a scarecrow is waiting, drenched in sun, but shivering. The summer fields swept away behind him, dry and bare.

'Don't get your feet wet,' he said sarcastically.

'I am not a thief,' she sighed, 'I will not steal your wife. I am not your cold twin, your glittering leaf bud, am I?'

He did not answer. She looked at him and predicted twilight in several languages.

'You smell of dry rot,' he said spitefully, 'it is your death I smell.'

Then the ghost jumped on him, got hold of him. Her wet hair! He almost screamed, pushed her away, throwing her back into the stream. She came at him again, the sodden ghost, and grabbed him. He pushed at her again but his heart wasn't in it. She threw her whole weight at him and they both fell to the ground and she slid his hand up between her legs. He expected cold dead flesh but she was warm. It was a hard decision for him to make and he hesitated. She said, 'I'll rechristen you, dear.' He was trembling and his lanky prick quivered, a lady killer. He rubbed himself up against her blue skirt and touched his wary sex with his right hand. She was silent, she was reconstructing signals for his flesh. But she felt no pleasure. There was no sensation in her cunt, ever. Dead. To him it felt warm, because she intended him to feel a warmth, but to her it was like clay, her dead sex, cold and unamplified. Theron was gasping and fingering her hairy ghostly cunt. Even though he knew this was a hoax, he glanced around to make sure no one was watching, not a soul, and unfastened his pants. He gestured to Vellet and she laughed. They both rolled on the bank of the stream.

He looked at her face and forgot she was dead, a pool of stagnant water. Almost soberly he embraced her. She shifted her body and thought, yes, he is playing the giant excellently.

It was nearly midsummer and he mounted her unhesitatingly in the warmth of noon. His penis travelled slowly at first through waves of a remote fire. Vellet hitched her legs up higher. She grimaced like a grotesque doll when he entered her, squinting, twisting her mouth. She had no pleasure to gain. He moved faster, bewitched. She felt nothing in her cold place, no rift, no gulping ache, no orgasm, no absolution. He pushed into Vellet hard and holy, approaching the pure colour of a clear sky in his body and his mind. His body was shining around him and before his eyes she was glowing, a moist tumult. He could already taste orgasm, feel it, talk to it, love it, press against the mother-of-pearl strength of it – and then there is just the echo of Vellet's laughter and his penis plucked out of a woman's body that had never been there and he moved his closed hand fast over his penis and heaved once or twice, groaning slowly and it came out stark and whinnying, no longer beautifully pent but slimy, uncanny. He crouched on the bank of the stream feeling the watery air on his body and he heard the echo of her laughter, merry and horrid, smelt the odour of decay she'd left behind. The violent memories of his first marriage stank in his nose. He cursed her, the ghost of veins. He remembered how she drowned, like a wooden doll denying he possessed any part of her. Her husband, the darkest possible bugger, stands in the shadows and does not dive into the river to rescue her. He hears her cries but does not want to rescue her. The other man also turns away from the drowning woman. This is the frequently recurring image in Theron's mind. How he watched but did not move, watched, as if his hand were poised over a table containing sharp surgical instruments.

The little wooden hands splinter and bleed thin sap. A writhing dolly weeps, confesses her infidelities. A woman drowns. Men walk away from the scene of the tragedy.

On this summer day, he grovels beside the stream amid the scum of his seduction.

THIRTEEN

BETH in a sunless room, standing at a window, watching summer fail.

Why do I exhaust myself thinking of Ash and of the past? Why am I wrenching my life out of shape? If I could forget Ash, I would be better able to help Theron and leave no dirt in our lives.

Theron walks slowly across the lawn, carrying a basket. He is going to fetch apples from the orchard. Beth watches him. The shadow of Ash grows thinner but still maims me. I fear the thought of her more than the armies of Arabia and Abyssinia.

Bridge-building. That is what Theron and I must learn. We must exchange confidences. That solemnity with which he speaks of the dead Vellet! What does it conceal? Theron and I must be helpmates, not enemies. In this chill summer, our marriage is turning into an icy circus without clowns and where we are the trapezists, strong men, acrobats on horseback, lion-tamers. It cannot continue like this. Theron goes about with such a serious look, as if heavy responsibilities were all he thought of, as if he'd been charged with the task of writing the gospels out in letters of gold.

Beth does not know that for Theron there is always the woman walking in the fields, always the woman slowly advancing towards him, offering him broken bread, broken sex. He turns away, he will not eat the dead woman's food.

Beth grumbled to herself a little longer before she made up her mind. Then she ran outdoors, across the lawn, through the air too cool for June. She found Theron in the orchard, murmuring a short and hurried prayer over a huge collar of fungus growing on an old apple tree.

'Isn't it magnificent,' he said. He looked happy and stroked the fungus.

'But there aren't many apples,' she said.

'No,' he agreed, 'it's too early.'

This conversation relaxes them both and they walk companionably through the little trees. But Beth is still trying to decipher all his silences, his casual remarks. She watches him as if her eyes were mirrors.

'Are you afraid of me?' he said suddenly, harshly.

'No,' she said evenly, 'no. Afraid for you.'

'Ah,' he said, and laughed. 'Afraid for me, in the fields and meadows of my burning.'

'Why are you burning, Theron?'

At the orchard gate, they face one another, the basket tilted on the grass, the few apples green and sour.

'Let me help you,' she said.

He shook his head.

'Soon I must meet the guardian of the necropolis, that master of mummification. I am strong, Beth, but not strong enough.'

'What are you struggling with . . .?'

He shook his head again. Between the branches of the nearest tree, Vellet is peering at them. He will not look at the ghost in the tree, but he winces.

'What are you afraid of?' asks Beth urgently. 'You must tell me soon or we shall be separated, driven apart by your fear. And by mine, for make no mistake it is contagious.'

'It might be best . . . for you to go away for a time . . . till I know if I can tell you. Until I am certain of my fear.' He speaks nervously, half smiling at her.

'Look, I don't want you to face your trouble alone,' she said.

'I don't want you to suffer because I'm tainted.'

'Tainted?' Beth is shocked. 'Tainted? By what, Theron?' She kisses him but he only submits to her touch, does not respond.

'I won't leave,' she said quietly, 'our marriage is a habitation I share with you.'

'But it can't be any good for you, nor can I,' he said desperately, 'not yet. If I can work this out for myself, then we'll be happy, then.'

'No,' said Beth, 'that is dangerous. I won't leave you.'

He looked at her and smiled but heard Vellet hiss.

'Don't hoard your unhappiness like a miser,' Beth whispers gently.

'I don't. Do I?' he answers, still smiling, tired.
'Tell me what taints you.'
'I can't,' he said, and shrugged, grinning sheepishly. He picked up the basket of apples. She caught at his arm.
'It is about Vellet, isn't it, all this,' she asked breathlessly, 'you feel guilty about her death, don't you, oh, but you know it was not your fault, you know that. You are relishing your damn guilt. Stop it! Let us live.'
She stops as if her throat is dismantling her. Her sudden anger is caught between an old warm moon and the ice of the new crescent. Summer whirls in the grey garden, freezing Beth and Theron to their fears. Then his obscene answer to her questions starts a long cry of pain in her head.
When she had spat the taste of it out of her mouth, he'd gone. She was in a silent landscape. Haunted? she thought. He is ill. Yet hesitation rises in her, she will not accept that he is sick. It is grief, she thinks, as she stumbles back to the house, the folds of her skirt heavy as timber. Her thoughts loop and twist and entangle her. The riddles? What does he mean? A ghost? Haunted? And that look of fear in him that Beth cannot lull.
As soon as Theron told Beth he was haunted, he had regretted it, and swore at her. Then he saw the girl with the goose in her arms hurrying towards him and Vellet drove him out of the garden, away from Beth.
Vellet leads him to the river and tells him, 'my fingers are locked to your sex.'
'Will I see this ghost?' Beth had asked, out of her shock.
'You saw her once,' he said, over his shoulder. And then he had gone. A harsh jog, a disjointed lope.

Where does the midwife live? On the highlands of the moon? Where does she live? I need her help. How am I to be born?
This is Vellet's question, after Beth has walked by her, unseeing. Vellet stood beside Beth as Theron stammered out his story and she thought, now Beth must see me! But Beth did not. Beth moved through the ghost, noticing nothing, no feather, no sediment of the phantasm.

The midwife's hand renews shadows like me, thinks Vellet. I look earthwards and I'm afraid. How am I to be planted again in warm flesh, how possess a spinal cord, a brain, blood, fibres and bundles of nerves? To feel my lungs heave with breath again, to be alive? I hear the songs of slow constellations, yes, I know the darkness of apples. I move quickly through the fiery cities. I study with the giant, hard lessons. But no one sees me. I am dead. I wander slowly through the snowy woods. No one sees me. I drift into summer. No one sees me but Theron. He sees me sometimes, not often. He closes his mind to me. I am the real nonentity. I want Beth to see me. Look at me, Beth. Turn to me. Drink my icewater. Beth, can you hear me? Beth. How many times must I ask you? Give him back to me, that man. He must take me to the midwife.

Beth hears Vellet's summons but she outlaws it. She mistakes Vellet's voice for the voice of Ash. The house echoes with Ash's voice. Beth hates Ash sometimes, and would inform against her, the accomplice. Leave me alone, she yells, and out of the corner of her eye a shrivelled little old man stood watching her and grinning.

Beth rushes from room to room, trying to shift the burden of Theron's confidence, but she cannot get away from it. It is an immovable thing now, the knowledge he has passed on to her, like an inheritance, a house or piece of land. She cannot dodge it. It casts its shadow.

Haunted! Is he crazy?

She is suddenly ravenous and stands in the kitchen gobbling thick slices of bread, lumps of cheese.

Ghost! How often does it appear? If there is a ghost, I'll capture it and tame it, that's a promise.

The food in her mouth is like raw flesh. Her thoughts are a network of painful legacies that she cannot untangle.

She comes to rest by the open window of her sitting room. She stares out at the rich fertile yet obscure light that falls on the garden and the hills beyond. My abundant possessions, she thinks angrily. Beth is a woman carried forward on a long swelling wave she cannot control. Yet her vigour remains with her. She will stay with Theron. She will not go to her safer house on the moor, not yet, not until there is nowhere else to go. She is a strict observer of her own rules. The sources of her strength are uncertain, but they serve her well.

The long melancholy of summer afternoons remains though, sunlit and with the voices of children calling from distances . . .

Beth sits by the window. Her book waits, unread. The piano waits, silent. The sun falls on the yellowing keyboard.

How can you subject me to such afternoons, Ash? How can you invent such blank hours for me, Theron?

Outside, the calm casual summer evening at last begins springing from the roots of an imperishable moon.

Even though he's left Beth fatigued and half unable to believe his confession – I'm haunted – he thinks of her as a stronghold. Her fortitude is my only chance, thinks Theron. He can find nothing to complain of in Beth. In his mind it is he alone who is guilty of the felony that is coming between them.

He has been running hard and is ready to drop. His limbs flail through the sites of summer. But he cannot outrun Vellet.

Theron rests at the boundary of a little coppice. Behind him, the young trees. Ahead of him, a rural skyline complete with cattle and ruined buildings. Also he observes, at the centre of this landscape, Vellet, the young dead girl. It could not be otherwise. Just as Vellet has not learnt how to release herself from her death, her husband has not learnt to be free of the crusade he is still organizing against Vellet. He calls her up, they are equal partners. But he will not acknowledge this, does not consider it. He walks towards Vellet. Her face is too harsh for a young girl and often it is invisible among shadows. Her death virginity rasps against her, against him. The wands of evening beat them both. He shivers. Vellet comes towards him. There's a luminous area all around her, like that produced by the application of pressure to an eyeball, by a finger, say.

'Tomorrow's my birthday,' she whispers.

He shrugged.

'How old will you be?'

The ghost shouted with laughter, then frowned like a stranger who has adopted women's clothing unlawfully.

'I miss music,' she said, 'I cannot hear music now. I always liked loud music. No cradle-songs or serenades for me. I liked loud music. I've asked that giant pinned to the hill to sing for me, but he won't. Hairless white giant. I hate him. I'm lonely, Theron.'

Then he looked at her as if he'd never seen the ghost before.

'Lonely,' he said, startled, and then smiling against his will, 'you mean you can feel that, loneliness?'

The ghost blushed.

A light summer rain fell on Theron as he sat by the roadside. The saplings in the plantation became more delicate, each leaf seemed handsewn in the rain. Theron stared at Vellet, puzzled. She stood by the plantation fence, her face turned away.

'So lonely,' she continued, 'I don't have flesh, Theron. I am a blue air of loneliness, my lips and tongue, my ear-lobes and eye-lids, clitoris and nipples are only shadows on the air. I am always cold. I have nothing to look forward to. I am locked in a small room of haunting. I cannot take the next step, I do not know how.'

After a moment, he said,

'I don't know how to free you either, Vellet.'

The ghost turned her head to look at him, hurt.

'Why did you let me drown, Theron?' Her voice is subdued.

'I hated you,' he replied immediately.

'Yes,' she said, 'I understand.'

'I could not lift a finger to help you that night,' he told her. 'And it has ruined us both. I followed you out of the house, I saw you meet your boyfriend, watched you, heard you arguing, saw him push you away from him, hard, heard you cry out, then saw you fall, gracefully, into the water. But I could not help you.'

'He did not help me either,' said Vellet, 'perhaps he hated me too.'

'Perhaps,' said Theron, pulling a leaf off the nearest tree.

'But I was so young,' she cried out.

'I loathed you,' he said, 'your presence in my house revolted me, I was going to turn you out, when you drowned I was glad to be rid of you, it was something I was wholeheartedly in favour of.'

'But you are not rid of me, my dear.'

'Not yet.'

'You never will be, believe me.'

When he turned to answer her, she had gone, the rain was heavier, the sunlight slanted through it, broken.

'I will be rid of you,' he said. 'This haunted husband will exorcise you.' He heard his heart beating, simple rhythm. Fear left him, briefly. Laplandish summer, he thought, and walked on smartly to get warm.

That evening Beth climbs Giant Hill, resisting changes in the weather.

I saw her! That night; the ghost in Church Street, accosting Theron. I saw her. I do not want to see her again. I don't want to walk on any wet paths prepared by a ghost.

She is sitting very still on the shoulder of the Giant. The night comes, like a door closing.

Theron is in his garden, moving among the long spikes of flowers.

Darkness bleeds into the moon-rise and turns the sheets of all the beds scarlet. Beth is an old moon kept in the deepest recesses of the sky. The giant's forefinger is nine inches long. His eyes of chalk are blind. Who gave birth to him? His mother was a pioneer, mistress of the landscape, labouring among stones.

I could detach the smiles from Vellet's face, thinks Beth grimly. I could throw her smile down the well. Why should I be afraid? Anger floods Beth, almost uncontrollable. Your hooves are silent, Vellet. Where are you?

But tonight Vellet is afraid of Beth and hides on the other side of the giant.

So is there a dead woman? thinks Beth. Or does Theron wallow in some dream? Some nightmare he wants to put on me? Breathe your uncanniness on me, Vellet!

But the ghost does not come to Beth. The ghost's flowers are bleeding.

Theron opens his eyes to a vista of scented alphabets. He is looking for Beth in the garden and cannot find her. His empty skin flaps in the breeze and the night steadily tightening around him appals him. He glances up at the moon that reminds him of Vellet and he is afraid again. He is soaking with sweat. Where can I escape? Go abroad? No. The answer is here. I have no bullets, bombs or torpedoes to destroy Vellet. I can only end the haunting by remaining here, keeping a close watch on her, the ghost, and bearing with this fear. He blunders out of the garden and down the lane, looking for Beth.

Beth's limbs are stiff. She gets to her feet, stands at the hilltop and lets the moon flash its messages upon her and the moon-white giant. Beth thinks of her heart coiled like a shell. She watches the giant and sees his white ribs rise and fall with the breath of the night. She hears the voice of the giant, stressing her name.

'I am listening, Giant.' Her voice is quieter than her shadow.

'Listen, Beth. That woman, so suggestive of waterfalls, the woman who haunts, she needs help.'

'Help?'

'Your help.'

'Why?'

'Show her how to travel her death and then she will be free to start again. She will no longer haunt your man.'

Beth is rebellious and speaks raucously.

'And how am I supposed to accomplish this?' There is a sigh like ice from the white mouth of the giant.

'I don't know. I only know it is from you the knowledge will come.'

Beth is about to reply angrily again but stops, hears those harsh words drop away into the night like stones into deep water.

'Will Theron be free?'

'If Vellet is freed, yes.'

'Where is Vellet now?'

'She is stroking her body beneath the water. She will not visit tonight. Listen. You do not need to outwit Vellet, it is not that kind of solution. You must understand her, contemplate her.'

Beth's body is clammy, she hears her blood clatter, and fears that her time of albino orgasm is past. This is a problem of different dimensions and brings fear shining brightly through Beth. She moans as if flames surround her and pulls at her hair with her fingers.

'Giant, where's your whip, your other torturing instruments.'

'No, I am not a monster. I am a prisoner of this hill. I wish to get up and walk, to be made of flesh, not chalk. But unlike Vellet there's no way for me to move on. I am to be here always, I know. I am in pain here. A great hammer vibrates in my skull. All darkness is here for me to consume with my white vigilance. I am the guardian of ghosts, Beth, and I am lonely, shunned, and too close to earth and sky. I have no black wings. I cannot escape. I have no doors to close behind me. I must stay on this hill, watching the world with my blindness.

Beth is within the giant's domain and says,

'I will try to help.'

She tries to recall the face she'd glimpsed in Church Street but her memory is too frail: the lines of Vellet's face twist like snakes, shading in abnormalities. Beth sees a skull that dances, a caterwauling mouth.

'But black wings brush at me,' she said to the Giant. There was no answer. 'Fool,' she told herself, 'staying out half the night, getting chilled, talking to yourself.' But she is reluctant to go back home. She stares across the valley at the fields of wheat on which the moonlight glints. The fields are webs rocking in the wind. Beth has been so deeply embedded in her own life these past weeks that she has not noticed the wheat growing, ripening.

Now Beth feels large and heavy. In the pale askew moonlight she has a strange shadow. She lifts her hands from her sides and snuffs up the odours of the hill, damp and vegetative. In her mind's eye she sees her own downcast reflection. She presses her right hand against her left. The boorish behaviour of her husband cannot be explained by a ghost! He is hoodwinking me. Beth's jaw aches with tension, her eyelids feel dead, her thoughts are a whirlpool of little wet lips. Silence comes at her without warning, hurtling towards her and the soft pulpiness of fear sickens her.

The giant inhales the innuendoes of the girl descending his steep slope.

He looks down at the village.

The giant knows there is no such thing as an easy death.

The giant plays no card games.

The giant wears no loin cloth.

The giant sings of his blindness.

He breaks the evil bride's neck.

He has no name, he does not drink blood.
The giant looks at the hour-glass.
He plucks his own heart out, gazes at it, replaces it, roaring with laughter.
The unworldly giant stammers. Easter candles blaze with light. He puffs them out.
The giant haṣ no harlot.
The giant awaits the return of the ghost with mud on her skirt and waterweed in her womb.
He settles to sleep: the galactoid gaps in his memory must be repaired.

Hoodman-blind, Theron moves through the empty village. In the back of his mind is an idea unclear and indistinct that frightens him. A few lights glow in bedrooms and sitting-rooms. He pauses outside one house. Should he go in and speak to someone? As he hesitates, his hand on the gate, the light goes out. He drags himself on down the street. It is his loneliness that makes him ungainly. He longs for company. The ghost does not trouble him tonight. Her drugged starfish face does not loom towards him. But he is so tired, he hardly values the respite. The moon makes grey staircases in the sky that turn white and move with an appearance of truth. He shambles on. A dog barks somewhere and then a child cries in one of the cottages. The grey hulk of the church does not interest Theron. He wanders by, not looking at the graveyard. The son of god, thinks Theron, feeble creature, with his long pointed shoe, what son, what god? But there was no passion in Theron's complaint. He has his mind on other matters.

He hurries along the lane as if to a consummation. The little stream flows quietly at his side. He is walking and looking back over his shoulder, unaware of doing so. He remembers his dream the previous night: I am sitting at a devil's table and my mouth is dry as a diamond. I am very hungry and very thirsty. I ask for food and drink, in a voice that means what it says. The black folk bring me my fare. They set it out on the devil's table; drowned mice, drowned cats, drowned dogs. And I must eat. I eat. I bellow like a child. Two women come running, their hair loose, their voices crooning anciently, the juice of ripe fruit running from the corners of their mouths. And then I woke.

The path brings him to a wooden bridge across the stream. He waits here, hare-lipped by the moonlight. His anus itches. At length he saw a shape moving through the trees on the other side of the water, shape of a woman in a long skirt, hair loose. But he cannot tell which wife it is.

'Beth?' he calls nervously. 'Beth?'

'Yes, it is me.' Her voice is a remedy for him. He smells the amphibian odour of her sex. He sets foot on the bridge. She meets him halfway. They embrace like refugees and fend off the night that carves its initials in their flesh.

They walk home together, slowly, through the moonlit village, and they promise themselves that the days of easy anger are over.

This promise is like a narrow strip of land between two seas, under constant threat.

FOURTEEN

MENAGERIE of unopened letters.

Beth watches the postman trudge down the muddy track. She stoops, gathers up the circulars, bills, two postcards, a letter addressed to her, from Tabitha. Beth rips this open, scans it quickly, frowns, screws the envelope up and tosses it in the rubbish basket. Tabitha is back from her visit to London. Beth puts the rest of the mail on Theron's desk.

Ash writes me no letters! I ache between two extremes, two ghosts, women I cannot catch hold of, cannot meet. His ghost and mine. His and hers.

Summer shadows fall on Beth through the frosted glass of the front door. From the radio left on in the kitchen, a throbbing of lickspittle music.

Ash, my nature's sister, recollection of you is brief and blinding. I fear your shape-shifting, even from so far away, so long ago. I still find myself adopting, practising your gestures, your facial expressions. In the place where love is legally coined, you dog my footsteps, and make me ask myself, what am I doing here, living with a man as haunted, more haunted than I, so that Theron and I are made of one colour, no contrasts: dark molecule of our marriage. What will happen to us?

Ash was running across the field. She was obeying the brackishness of the day. It was the last time I saw her. Ash . . . We won two out of the three games, but the third game we lost. When Jake said, I guess it's time to be on our way, you said *yes* to him and not to me. The continuous sound of your name, Ash, Ash, Ash . . . I can't get away from it, and now it's becoming like an impurity in the blood.

You went away with him. He'd learnt a lot on his travels and you needed to be taught. He was wealthy, he was sensual: did he remind you a little of your first 'lover', Ash, the one who took you from the city to witness the spectacle of his onanism? Jake gave you more than that, I suppose, but you never write to tell me about your life now.

Beth does not like to think about these events, the meeting of Ash and Jake. She prefers to believe that they left only a slight trace on her life, that she was not wounded deeply. Ash and I had a summer, she thinks, there was no way of making that last, and neither of us wanted it to, not that much. Tougher needs arose in us both. Yet that summer still haunts me, encloses me, obsesses me.

It was in the autumn that Jake arrived, bringing change. He and Ash were married at Christmas. I lived in the house all winter and all spring, alone, as if it was a membraneous bag or pouch in which I curled. One day at the beginning of the next summer I was in the market town, browsing in a little bookshop, when a man, who looked vaguely familiar, introduced himself to me. He was a lecturer at the university, in the history department, and we had met once at a college dance. He asked me if I'd like a coffee in the restaurant next door. I said yes, off we went together, and so Theron and I met. It was a comfort, to talk to someone, be with someone. He seemed calm, easy to get along with, our friendship developed, eventually we married. Ash and Jake did not come to our wedding, though they sent an elaborate gift. Ash has not written since.

One morning I thought I saw Ash hanging from a tree, her virtues spattered with blood, but it was just a shadow.

Beth sits down at the kitchen table to write her grocery list. She has a slight burn on the index finger of her left hand where she caught the hot oven door yesterday.

In the sunny kitchen she is a dark abrupt silhouette, as if left behind by the rain.

Sun skirts through the village gardens.

The giant grows whiter against the summer green of the hill, against the blue of cloudless sky. All the ghosts play slapstick games in the summer. Beth lifts her head. She thought she heard someone speaking in the next room. But all is quiet. She stares at the calendar on the wall, at the girl naked but for boots and parachute.

Last night Beth and Theron met on the bridge and became

entangled, bodies driven together. In their watertight bedroom, they blushed, forming a complicated sexual pattern, pressing their wet hot faces together, discovering ultimately a composure of flesh. Beth stares at the wall, considering last night's complicities: husband, giant; giant, husband. Even from herself, she keeps secret the extent of the pleasure she experienced last night, as Theron curved inwards, reaching deep inside her. The compass of her delight seems like a warning now.

She stares at her hands folded on the table. Her hands glow, as if part of a great conflagration. But was Jake right, to accuse me of letting Ash fall asleep in my world? Was she a sort of sleeping beauty, as he said? Was he right? Was I suffocating her? Was my body like the scum of molten metal, harming Ash? When he accused me of that, almost lightly, but with such accurate timing and inflexion, letting his power fall delicately upon Ash, he convinced her.

Yet, a few days before the final break, she ran from me across those fields, as if running from Jake also.

But she went with him, and my life became ... unfinished ...

Ash is sitting in an armchair by the window, sewing a button on her yellow blouse. Beth is kneeling by the fire, bending over a book. The man stands at the open door, smoking a cigarette and watching the birds wheel and caw above the evening lawn. The sky darkens, clouds take on priapic shapes. Beth glances up at the man, suspiciously.

God with his long sharp knife carves the moon-meat of the women and they bleed.

Both women are menstruating. Ash is bleeding heavily, she is at the beginning of her period. Beth is on her last day and the towel between her legs is hardly stained.

Beth rises to her feet. She longs for her body and for the body of Ash to turn to gold. She wants this man, with his dangerous outspoken demands, to freeze, to congeal into iron.

Ash looks up from her sewing, glances angrily at Beth. Ash does not look at Jake. The blood of virginity has visited her unexpected;

she was not due for another week. It is the tension, the fight between Beth and Jake, with her as the prize, that has brought her period on.

She has shared this summer with Beth, living at her house. It has been a summer of deft mornings and wooded afternoons. Ash had seen the little hand-written advert in the post-office window, room to let, and that same evening rang Beth's number. They met the next morning and took to one another at once. It has been a summer of long walks, of bathing in the river, of gardening. They spent their evenings reading, or playing the piano and singing together. Since that first afternoon, sitting on the lawn, when Beth reached out and touched Ash, plunging headlong into an echo, the sound and shape of one woman has been reflected in the other. They have had a summer of blossom, egg and ache: identical creatures. Until the summer day with a sky coloured like a long snaky fish, an eel, the man interrupted their life. Ash wonders if she is depleted by her experiences with Beth, if she might not now prefer the man's riddle to the woman's. She is very careful to avoid looking at Jake as he stands in the doorway, but the blood thrusting out of her with such great vitality warms her. What Beth offers seems scanty. She thinks of the other man, who brought her out of the city. She remembers his stumpy penis rearing up. She bites off the thread of her sewing cotton.

Beth frowns. Jake watches her calculatingly, like a moneylender. He stubs out his cigarette. He walks across to Ash. She does not look at him.

'Ash,' he says.

Ash looks at Beth. Beth bends over her book. She will not help.

'What is it, Jake?' Her voice is unsure, Ash, a scarlet spider in her throat. Jake smiles, looks out of the window at the evening sky and the clouds grown warty, like a muster of witches.

I have lost, thinks Beth, not moving, not defending her claim, it is Jake's evening, and the embarkation of Ash amid leaves and moons.

Jake touches Ash on the shoulder.

'Come out for a walk, Ash. Come on,' he said.

They all remember the fierce argument this morning, Jake and Beth shouting at the tops of their voices in the white room. The way Beth pranced about the room, hysterical. How Jake had been very calm, very decided. How Ash had watched, and listened: and looked sulky because she was frightened. Jake speaks of our kind of love as knowledgeably as a fisherman who never saw a fish, Beth had sneered. Do you want his wet embrace, Ash? she had cried. But Ash kept silent. The stench of flames bursting between Jake and Beth was too acrid for her, she couldn't breathe, and she barged out of the room with an angry embarrassed grin, leaving Beth and Jake staring at each other, their gestures callous and mediocre, filling them with disgust.

But now, evening: Jake touches Ash on the shoulder, lightly, lovingly. Ash gets up, smiles at him, then leads the way out into the garden. He follows her without glancing at Beth.

Beth has lost. She is lost. She bends over her book. She is a young woman with a wooden heart and she knows what the interior of her rectum looks like. Also she knows that Jake asked Ash to wear her red dress this evening and that Ash had refused, pointing wordlessly to the red flowers in the garden. My uninterrupted possession of happiness is over.

That evening, Ash and Jake walk slowly through the lady-crab shadows of Beth's garden. Ash thinks, the hound was petrified with the vixen, to end their perpetual chase.

'Beth was struck by lightning as an infant,' says Jake. Ash stared at him doubtfully.

'It's true,' he said. 'It was a miracle she survived.'
'So I imagine,' she answered slowly.
'I don't imagine Beth will ever get married,' he said.
'Because of the lightning?'
'Yes.'
Ash smiled.
'The dream sees through you, Jake.'
'What do you mean?' he flared up. He turned to her angrily, they stood by the greenhouse, the half-moon was reflected in the darkening panes of glass.
'What do you mean?' he asked again, more quietly.
'I mean, Jake, that what you say awake is different from what you say asleep.'
'And what do you think I say when I'm asleep.'

'Different things.'

'Will you ever find out what they are? Will you ever listen, as I sleep?'

'You must remember them yourself,' she said tartly. Her hands ache to touch wood. His hand touched her throat, her breasts. The blood hummed between her legs.

'You're full of tricks and artifice,' he said, 'Beth taught you those. I'll teach you other things.'

Ash says nothing and tries to think of suns and starfish, but instead the story of a girl comes into her mind, the girl who walked along the suburban avenue pushing a yellow pram packed full of dynamite. In the shadows she sees old hands of bronze gathering up the night.

Jake leads her into the greenhouse. She stumbles and falls against him. He supports her. There is the odour of warm earth and tomatoes. In the summer Beth and Ash often worked in here. At the far end, there's a pile of old sacks. Ash looks down at them. She hears the native language of the stars, twisty and mournful, but she cannot utter any antidote. She gasps at Jake's oaths, his suggestions, his pledged words. The river is the wet tongue of the giant. Ash's dress is a biblical blue. She is lying on the sacks, dry and rough against her skin and the earth smell is strongest here. The moon sees her. The moons know.

'Ash,' the man said, touching her. He stretches at her side. She whispered to him, 'I'm bleeding . . .' 'I know . . .' he answered, 'it doesn't matter.' He began to stroke her, calmly, easily.

'With your body, you could walk into church naked and marry me like that.'

'No, don't say that,' she tells him, 'I don't want to marry naked.'

But she is nearly naked, with the blood flowing. The blue dress lies alone. Night shines against the fox sleep of Ash's breasts and night freezes in the ice of her pubic hair. His fingers comb through her earthy hair. She touches his penis clumsily.

She says, 'I am clean.'

He laughs, low in the darkness. She smiles in the dark. Her breasts sting. She raises her knees. She watches his jagged shadow snared in the moonlight. He snuffs up her brine and eases himself into her warm red virgin cunt. Her blood makes her first time easier. He is an early settler in new country. She begins to make dark cries. The penis moving in her is like an unexpected obstacle which both wounds and sensitizes her. He lifts himself and shudders, reading her body's alphabet. She spells out his. They'll learn of their imperfections in the future but now every second is valid, blossoming. On the ground, lying in the dirt, she tastes the kiss of the giant preserved in Jake's mouth, and moans when the itch-ache of virginity is suddenly sluiced and she is made open, elastic in orgasm. Frosty fire licks her lips. This is the married bonfire. Her blood and his spunk marry together.

When they return to the house, it saddens them, this couple, the lovers, to see Beth's face grimacing, the hack-work of a dauber.

Yes, they returned to my house, hesitating, their clothes dirty, and both of them, stumbling, half-asleep. Next morning, they packed up and went. For Ash, it was the best thing. They are still together, I suppose. I wish she'd write and tell me how she is. But she does not write. Not in one of seven languages, not one. Beth sits stiffly at the table, an old address book in her hand, her mind clouded by imaginations of that first coupling: Ash and Jake.

Beth is afraid to write another letter to Ash, afraid of the silent rejection, or, worse, a scribbled postcard that says less than nothing.

'I am not strong enough,' Beth muses, turning away from the picture she had made of the lovers.

In a half-shadow doorway, Vellet watches Beth. If I whisper now, she thinks, Beth might hear me. But Vellet is not ready to speak to Beth yet. She watches from the shadows, her freshwater fingers and thin buttocks hunched in warfare. A stingless shadow.

Odours of iodine rise from the garden where rain has just fallen.

Beth tastes her own ghost.

Ash! she trembles. I am following you through a sewer. Should I rename you Cloacina? Or is that my name?

'Can you translate my name into Latin, Beth?' said the voice in the blue doorway.

Beth whirled round, turned sharply, just in time to see the apparition fade, the face made nomadic by death, the watery lace at neck and wrists . . .

'You!' she cried.

But then was silent.

Theron is coming downstairs. He is whistling and looks very relaxed. The sound of the guns reverberates against the windows of the house. Men are shooting rooks or rabbits beyond the common.

'Over in Hare Coppice, from the echo, and the distance,' said Theron.

'Think so?'

'Yes. There, or maybe even as far away as Well Field.'

Look! There again. Vellet is smiling at Beth. Beth squints at the sunlight, at the muggy air. But Theron cannot see Vellet. The ghost steers her tissue shadow out of his reach.

'Beth? Beth!'

'Yes. Sorry, I was miles away. What did you say?'

'I said, it is not pleasant to be shut in a cage, but believe me, I am trying to get free.'

'Yes, Theron.' Beth smiles and embraces her husband. 'Yes, Theron, I know. Between words, between gestures, we are rediscovering ourselves.'

'Last night . . .' he kissed her gently.

'Yes,' she agreed happily, 'it was lovely.'

Looking happier than he had for weeks, Theron got his fishing gear together and went out. But the shadow of the saboteur has fallen on Beth. Vellet covets Beth's fields and blue fathoms of ease, her calmness.

'But ghosts are out of fashion!' said Beth aloud. There was no answer. Beth sighed and got on with her housework. Polishing the first wife's furniture! While she was dusting, it seemed to Beth she saw Vellet again, the room was like the room of an annunciation. The ghost looked sideways at Beth, giggled, spat and vanished.

FIFTEEN

WEASEL woman in the shelter of the rain.
Today is an unlucky day for the woman with her aching haunted head. She walks slowly, as if dragging havoc behind her. The rain shuns her. Beth hears the cry of wild geese; a mated pair, necks outstretched, fly above her, towards the sea coast. The sound grates upon her for she is distrustful of everything this morning.
She walks without seeing the landscape, skimping the horizon.
It had seemed to Beth that things had been improving, that she and Theron had drawn closer together in their trouble, sharing it. When he'd told her he was haunted by Vellet and they had talked at length about the ghost, penned the apparition up in simple words, descriptions, rationalizations, Beth had believed that their marriage, contracted carelessly by her, unwisely and obstinately by Theron, might blossom into at least a working allegiance: that there might be a way for them both to move out of jeopardy. But after her initial encouragement, after his original outburst and the strength and power of their love-making that night of their meeting on the bridge, there has been a withdrawal again. He has grown secretive and silent. The coldness of a flimsily constructed life has begun again. All week an inaudible conflict has been developing between them. He turned away from me, Beth insists to herself, it was him, not me. But she cannot deny that she has been shut up in her own private world, where Ash reigns. So have I not given him enough of myself? Has he sensed that I have another allegiance, a ghost of my own that I haven't entered in our log-book? Does this give me an unfair advantage over him?
The field hedges smell of the rain. Beth breathes in the green air, stares across at the giant veiled in fine rain. The sight of the giant adds to her irritability.
It is hard for Beth to believe what she saw last night. Are we sharing hallucinations, Theron and I? she thinks. She had awoken

suddenly, out of a neighing dream, soaked in sweat. Her thoughts were great blocks of stone crushing her. It was very dark, timeless, no moon. She was alone in the bedroom. She switched on the bedside lamp and glanced around the neat bedroom. The door was open. Her dream, details of which eluded Beth, had frightened her and, despite the return of their estrangement, she wanted Theron's company. I suppose he couldn't sleep again, she thought, and slipping on her dressing-gown she went downstairs.

It was when she reached the foot of the stairs that she heard the groaning begin and the sound touched her smooth skin like vomit.

The sound is coming from Theron's study. It is not a groan of a man in pain. Beth has heard this sound before, on other nights, less dark than this. Beth approaches the door of his study, she cannot help herself. A chill voice is repeating words in her ear – I see the lichen-scars, the river-scars on your face . . .

The door is open and in the candle-lit room Theron is abandoning his kingdom. He is sprawled, half-dressed, in an armchair, almost like a hostage, and there is a stink of rancid water in the room. Theron groans again and for an instant the Vellet ghost materializes, her incubus mouth clamped over Theron's penis, which is pointing erect towards death. He groans again with pleasure and writhes in the chair while Beth watches, stunned and sad.

Who will help Beth? Her brother the giant lives far away, over many mountains, and she does not like his advice. Beth stands in the doorway, remote and sad as a wave. Vellet is invisible at the moment, but Beth smells the foul gas of her presence in the room. Theron gives a final moan and the spurt flies up in the air, a white arc, and he sags down in the chair, eyes closed, satisfied.

Vellet puts her hand on Beth's shoulder. Beth feels the cold seep through her robe, numbing her. Beth shudders but forces herself to stare into the pretty and unspoilt face of the drowned woman.

'Almost every night,' whispers Vellet, 'when night burns its beautiful fire, I come to him and lead him towards my mouth, or my hand, or my sex.'

Beth looks around the familiar room, recognizing nothing. There is no help, not from books, paintings or flowers. She must remain and listen to the confidences of the ghost.

'I am his wife,' coos Vellet, 'and his sex is mine. I have him, Beth! There's not much left for you, is there?'

Beth blushes. Now she knows she has a rival, one she cannot sue for divorce, one she cannot assassinate. This is why Theron does not want to make love to her. Beth's cunt froths with jealousy, she is toppling backwards down a twisting staircase. She does not know how to answer, how to respond to her husband's mistress. Or is it wife? Or hallucination? Or are we both crazy, Theron and I? Is it a ghost that beckons to us and divides us, or is it our own failure to love that confronts us, dressed up as Vellet?

'You should call Theron Mr Blindman,' laughs Vellet. 'He cannot see past me.'

If I answer her, thought Beth, it will be nothing more than the untruths of brides exchanged defiantly.

Who will help Beth? Can a ghost be inseminated? she wonders, in a sudden fright.

'No,' hisses Vellet, answering Beth's unspoken question, 'no.' And her face looms like countless pryings before Beth, bringing bad luck. Beth hurls silence at the ghost and because of Beth's strength and her living blood Vellet flinches.

'I am still his bride, Beth.'

Then the ghost is gone. Beth did not see her vanish. Perhaps a slight glow pastelled against the wall; perhaps one candle was the beacon through which Vellet disappeared.

Beth stoops over Theron, to comfort him, to seek comfort herself, but he shakes her off angrily.

'Did you hear?' asks Beth.

'Hear what?'

'I was talking to Vellet.'

Theron fastened his pants and laughed bitterly.

'Talking to Vellet! My, you are making progress, Beth.'

Beth hesitated, then said nervously, tentatively,

'You feel it, then, do you? Really, when she touches you? Pleasure?'

He didn't answer.

'Doesn't the touch of Vellet feel cold, Theron?' He shook his head.

'No. No, it feels like a woman touching me.' Theron wavered, almost moved towards tenderness, but then his face grew harsh again and he determined not to make any excuses to Beth for his encounter with Vellet. It is not my fault, he thought. I am not to blame. I am the victim of these hauntings, when Vellet repeats the actions of past love-making. He scowls at Beth. But she is no longer frightened by his anger, the nature of his responses. It is Vellet she fears.

'How can it feel like a woman,' she persists, 'it is a dead thing. A dead thing,' she muses, speaking more to herself than to him.

'Christ, if I knew why it felt so real . . . I'd be happy,' Theron yelled, 'if I knew why I want it, it would not terrify me, stupid bitch!'

She swerved from the blow he aimed at her, and he made no further attempt to hit her. She took no notice of this violence, merely dodged it, and dismissed it. There are more important matters. She wonders if Vellet's ghosthood were fathomless, or whether there were limits, places where she/it might be made powerless. What laws govern Vellet? What exorcisms could be used?

'Now do you see,' he said desperately, 'what I meant by the haunting, by being tainted? How can we stay together when that thing, that perversion is my companion also?'

'Can't you protect yourself from . . . these . . . assaults?' Theron shook his head. 'Why do you think I wanted to remarry? I thought I would get free of it then.'

'But you are not free,' said Beth, shaken.

'No,' he said. Then he shrugged savagely and left Beth alone. She sobs once and the giant opens his eyes. Beth spits in the direction of the giant.

'You say I should help Vellet, Giant,' she cried, 'but how? Vellet is sucking the marrow of our marriage away, humiliating him, destroying me. How am I to help her?'

Then the silence and the darkness closed in on Beth.

Now on this rainy morning she walks into the village where all the streets are dirty. She passes the shops without stopping and enters the village church, pausing in the porch to tie a white scarf over her wet hair. She walks slowly towards the altar, her footsteps echoing on the stone pavement. The church is full of fear that belongs to Beth. The man approaches her as she sits in a devout attitude. His face is marked as by smallpox. She looked up at him and said, 'I want to walk in an unhaunted house, to have an unhaunted garden, an unhaunted man.' He said, 'Beth, you must try to arrange your thoughts without ambiguity.' She said to him, 'there is bad weather in the bible.' She spoke crossly. He said, 'listen. You can hear it? Time, ticking away? Decide. What do you want? To end the haunting? Or to understand the haunting?'

Beth cannot answer. Her silence is long and emaciated.

The man walks away.

Beth wanders through the back streets, past dustbins waiting for collection. The rain is deducing Beth's character from the shape of her skull. Beth knocks at a cottage door and is welcomed by her friend, Tabitha Irons, a small dark woman who smiles and speaks to Beth in a low rapid voice, leading Beth along a narrow hallway into a small brightly lit untidy sitting-room.

'I haven't seen you for ages, Beth,' she exclaims. Beth apologizes, smiles tensely.

'Is everything alright, Beth?'

Beth shrugs, does not answer. Tabitha hurries out of the room, calling back over her shoulder, 'take your wet things off and hang them to dry, Beth.'

Tabitha came back with the tea tray and the two women settle by the fire, drinking hot tea out of big chipped enamel mugs.

In the old days, Tabitha's cottage was traditionally owned by the village jailer and the portrait on the chimney breast, a faded daguerrotype, is that of the last jailer's wife. Upstairs, in the old chocolate box where she keeps her jewellery, mostly fake, Tabitha has a pair of gold ear-rings that belonged to this lady, given to her so that she would put in a 'good' vote at the election. But Tabitha is no descendant of jailers. She and her late husband bought the cottage from the great-grand-daughter of the last jailer. Tabitha never wears the election ear-rings, a present from the great-granddaughter, who had taken a fancy to Tabitha, but keeps them, as good luck emblems, belonging to the house, and keeping Tabitha in touch with the earlier occupants.

Tabitha is nearly ten years older than Beth. She is a widow and has lived in or near the village all her life. Irons had been a painter of some note. Upstairs in a locked room, five of his paintings remain, the five that Tabitha will not sell or exhibit. The first canvas is of a drunk woman womb-wounded, all shades of red. The second, a pair of long-necked griffons crouched by the pages of a treatise advocating sexual love. The third, and largest of the canvases, Jesus touching the veil of the Virgin. The fourth, Tabitha's favourite, the saint sipping blood, her face alight, and behind her, shadows like bruised armour. The fifth canvas, a portrayal of Tabitha and Harry as lovers, he rising through her like smoke, and, sheltering them both, the golden appletrees of the psalmist: lovers in an orchard. These are Tabitha's five icons. She cannot bear to let anyone in this room, except for the rarest occasions. Beth has been allowed to see these paintings once.

Tabitha is dark, hair and eyes nearly jet, and ornamented with necklaces, rings, brooches and bracelets which suit her more than they would most women. She wears long skirts, often with untidy hems, and there is a gypsy caravan feeling about her house. Tabitha is now not wife, nor virgin, nor mother: she is herself. She is outgrowing the pain of her widowhood and has little need of rewards. Her smile has many syllables.

Beth has confidence in Tabitha's wisdom. Tabitha sees how troubled Beth is, that a night horizon has torn her open, but she waits patiently for Beth to say what is wrong in her own time.

At first Beth keeps the conversation on a mundane level, sticking to safe topics, village gossip. Tabitha answers in the same language but watches Beth intently, seeing that Beth has worn sleep out. Yes, Beth is trying to wind her ghosts on to new spools. The voices of the women linger in the room, waiting for the storm to break over them. Tabitha is leaning forward, the flat palm of her hand unconsciously extended to offer Beth comfort. What is Beth thinking behind her calm conversation? In her mind she passes a rope set with thorns through her tongue and lets the blood drop on to her skirt. Beth's face is stark and reminds Tabitha of the black days of her own marriage, a man and a woman sharing frugal and bitter meals. She remembers Irons shoving her out of the cottage on a winter night. Wearing only her nightgown, she crouched shivering, beaten by a crowbar of solid silver, icy moonlight. She remembers crawling back into a terrible bed, wearing an iron collar, being fucked from behind, defenceless. Tabitha's wisdom has not come from an easy apprenticeship. She recalls the one-eyed husband who, even now, enters her dreams, commanding Tabitha to kiss unknown animals. So now she leans forward and touches Beth gently on the knee. Beth starts violently and catches her breath, thinking; Vellet!

'Whatever is it, dear?' asks Tabitha, worried.

Beth's lips twist from some sourness and she gets up, walks to the window. With her back to Tabitha she asks,

'Will we be of interest to archaeologists? Our bones, some day?'

'Yes, surely,' says Tabitha briskly, 'our bones will tell their stories.'

The moon is running backwards for Beth. She catches words in the folds of her skirt. Dark-odoured, she moves back to her chair, and tells Tabitha her story. The whispering of centaurs, that rain outside, and the thread of Beth's story moving through it.

'There is trouble between Theron and me,' she began.

'I feared as much,' said Tabitha.

'Tabitha,' she blurted out, 'I am jealous of Vellet. It is Vellet who is breaking up our marriage. She comes creeping out of some labyrinth and I am frightened of her power. She is taking Theron from me.'

Beth's voice is harsh, she is trembling with anger and fear. Her face is flaming with emotion. Tabitha lies back in her chair, eyes hooded, unshocked. She lights a cigarette. The little burning mist consoles Beth. Although she is not a smoker she breathes in deeply, with relief.

'Theron cannot put it behind him, then? Her death? He mourns for her still . . .?'

'No!' Beth jumps up from her chair. 'No, you don't understand.' Her voice breaks. To speak of Vellet and Theron denudes Beth. She is ashamed. She feels that it is she who is perverted, she who is the ghost. Her mouth is dry. Is this the summer, is this the frontier of my home, is this me? I am bungling my chance to get some support and advice from Tabitha.

But Tabitha does not find Beth's behaviour so strange. She sees how disturbed she is. She does not come forward to embrace Beth. She lets a gentle silence grow up between them and then she says, in her low voice,

'Come now, explain to me ... explain what I do not understand.'

Beth sighs.

'Explanations for this matter can only humiliate us both,' she says.

Now there is another silence between the women, who have both given up spinsterhood. Tabitha waits for Beth to reveal this mysterious indisposition, this anger about Vellet, a dead girl.

Beth wheeled round suddenly and came to kneel beside Tabitha.

'Tell me about Vellet,' she pleaded with the older woman, 'tell me something about her. I know nothing about her. I never bothered with village talk about her. But they did gossip about her, didn't they? Tell me. What sort of girl was she? Theron never talks about her. It is our forbidden territory. But what is she like?'

'Is?' queried Tabitha sharply.

'I'm sorry. I mean, what was she like?'

Tabitha touches Beth's hair, a sisterly gesture. Tabitha is unnerved by this insistence on Vellet. But she will not fail her friend. She realizes that Beth is approaching the kind of weariness that comes after repeated stress and knows that eventually such exhaustion will reduce Beth to a shadow, existing only among the uninvited guests in her skull. So, although the subject of Vellet is repugnant to her, Tabitha speaks, as Beth asked. Her voice grows deeper, her sentences are curt, she does not look at Beth.

'Vellet! Little tramp! That's what she was. She filled in her census form with misleading answers. Her lies were always hard to decipher. She was a skilled negotiator with dark things, the dark side, that one.'

'But you aren't lying to me, are you? Don't tell me lies.'

'It's the truth,' said Tabitha solemnly, 'I'm telling no lies, dear. When Theron married her, I was very worried for him. Unlike most of the villagers, the marriage did not surprise me. I knew he'd loved her for years, since she was a child, he told me so. But when I met him in the village soon after the marriage, I warned him, be on your guard. He laughed, I don't think he understood at all. Of course he was the only one who didn't know. The whole village knew about her tricks. She came to stay with me and Harry once, when she was a child. Spoilt! Expected to be waited on hand and foot. Even at that age, what was she, about twelve, she was trying it on with Harry . . .'

Tabitha got up and walked about the room, her memories of Vellet sucking at her, producing grating noises in her mind like unoiled hinges, and her hand on the door, opening, on to the tumbled room, Vellet's thin cry of fright, Irons' curse. Tabitha shivers.

Beth curled on the floor, says,

'Yes, what a cold summer.'

Tabitha does not answer. The pigments of pain, she thought, the little model with the saucy smile! Little Madam! Little Bitch! Better dead. Like Irons, better dead.

'And yet Theron never suspected Vellet, never knew she had other men . . .'

Tabitha shrugged and came back to her chair. She looked down at Theron's wife and crammed her own memories back into the dark. Where they belong, she thought. She shook her head slowly.

'Did he? I don't know. It's hard to say, Beth. Maybe towards the end he was beginning to catch on. She was out meeting one of her men friends the night she fell into the river, I'll be bound. Did you go to the inquest, Beth?'

'No. Why should I? I had troubles of my own at that time, and took no interest in village affairs.'

'Then you don't know she took drugs?'

'No. No, I never knew that. Was she high when she drowned?'

'Yes.'

'Poor Theron. How could he have been blind to all that?'

'He is a man who idealizes women. Or used to, he did Vellet. He never considered the possibility of her deviating from his vision of her.'

Beth looked into a future without light, in which she is exposed to peril. The palms of her hands are cold, damp. She knows she will not be able to make Tabitha understand about the ghost.

'Where did Vellet get her drugs from, Tabitha?'

'From her boyfriends. She took anything she could get. Why, I met her one evening, walking along the edge of Giant Hill and she lurched against me and said, "t-h-i-s r-o-a-d l-e-a-d-s t-o M-a-r-s-e-i-l-l-e-s. W-h-y d-o y-o-u w-a-n-t t-o t-r-a-v-e-l i-t? T-h-e i-s-l-a-n-d-s a-r-e c-o-v-e-r-e-d i-n i-c-e a-l-r-e-a-d-y?" Then she staggered on. I followed her, made sure she got home safely. Theron must have been away that night. I watched her reel into a dark house.'

Beth stretches her cramped limbs and shifts into a crosslegged position.

'You never told Theron?'

In her mind's eye, Tabitha sees Vellet, the naked model with the darkish pubic hair, the menace of her.

'No, I didn't. I realize now, maybe I should have done. But she was not one to call up compassion.'

Beth stares down at her clasped hands and thinks, once I could have lost a hand for a trivial offence. She glances up at the severe wife of the jailer, in the faded grey photograph. Beth will try now to explain the haunting to Tabitha.

'Tabitha, the real problem is that Theron blames himself for Vellet's death, it is making him ill and . . . he thinks . . . that is . . . I think . . . Vellet comes . . .'

Tabitha wrinkled her face and shook her head, interrupting Beth.

'No, Beth, no. Look, she was promiscuous, she was on drugs, she was unbalanced, out of control, out of anyone's reach. He's not at fault. He saw in her only what he wished to see, was blind to the rest, and she let him see only what he wanted, needed to see. He's not to blame.'

Beth looks helplessly about the room and her gaze comes to rest on a little work table of the utmost delicacy, its top surface mounted with a plaque of turquoise blue porcelain enriched with gold and painted animals. The beauty of this makes her weep, is the threshold of her weeping. She puts her hands over her face and sobs. Tabitha watches her, does not touch her, lets her alone.

'It's not often I'm like this,' gulps Beth. Her uncritical friend kneels beside her. The voices of the women reverberate.

'He says he is haunted, Tabitha! He says he sees Vellet's ghost. Haunted, he says he is haunted. He regards her as a person, a reality. He has sex with her, with Vellet, with the ghost, not with me!'

There is a code of grief in Beth's voice, an unbroken code, that silences Tabitha's immediate response.

'He cannot come near me most of the time, because Vellet won't allow him to come to me.' Beth weeps again, quietly.

Tabitha examines the irregular pieces of her thoughts.

'How long has he had this delusion?' she asks. Beth does not answer, she sobs harder and clenches her fists.

'Look, Beth dear, he must see a doctor, he is sick, very sick.'

Beth takes her hands from her face and howls aloud once, the cry of the cheated interpreter.

'God, Tabitha, then I am sick also, for I've seen her. She speaks to me also. She touches me. I find her long dark hairs in Theron's bed, on my bedroom floor, inside my purse, in the bath: and neither Theron nor I are dark, we are both fair. So I am sick, and crazy too, Tabitha! Me too!'

The two women stand at the doorway with subdued smiles, saying goodbye. Beth is very pale. Despite washing her face in cold water, it is obvious she has been crying. She has failed to convince Tabitha that Vellet's ghost is tormenting Theron and herself. She has failed to convey the reality of the ghost. She has had to agree with Tabitha's explanations, that she is overwrought, yes, tired, afraid of shadows, searching out far-fetched excuses to cover up the difficulties in her marriage. Yes, yes, she agreed with Tabitha, to silence her friend's gentle banalities.

Tabitha was out of the reach of ghosts. Common sense is her strong point.

'Look, you must have a long talk with Theron,' she urged Beth, 'get him to see a good psychiatrist, for heaven's sake. He's infecting you with his delusions. He is using the ghost motif to veil his sexual inadequacies, Beth.'

Beth nods obediently. What else can she do? She cannot penetrate Tabitha's defences. The two women kiss goodbye and Beth walks down the street, suddenly aware of being childless. She turns at the corner and waves back to Tabitha who stands watching in her doorway, watching her friend carefully, as if Beth were an invalid who might fall down in the street.

Beth waves again, then turns the corner. She acknowledges to herself that Tabitha is a wise woman but she overestimated

Tabitha. Her wisdom does not touch on ghosts. The ghost will not reflect itself in Tabitha's mirrors. Tabitha knows no exorcisms. She is not trained in such matters. So I must solve the matter myself, thinks Beth.

She stands at the thresholds, in the empty street, in the cutaneous rain.

Thresholds? which way for her?

One way leads to the river, another to the Giant.

The river is the place from which unwanted creatures rise in an uprush of blue, foetal, obstinate. The Giant is where these creatures might hide. Beth thinks of a bedstead covered with fresh clean white sheets, woollen blankets and soft pillows, and of a man who will embrace her, after he has washed his hands.

She sets her foot on the uphill path, away from the river, through the twilight towards the Giant.

SIXTEEN

The giant never tells lies.

Do I lie? Beth wonders. No, it is my dumbness that ruins summer, not my lies. If I knew the word that would disperse Vellet! Understand her, the giant said, understand her. How can I understand her? I want to obliterate her! How can I understand the ghost of a drugged and whorish girl?

Beth struggles on up the muddy lane. The moon is also a girl kept prisoner in a grey tent. Vellet rises now from her flowerless grave and begins to search the marshes for the embryo she lost there.

I couldn't explain it to Tabitha, I couldn't get it across to her! The thoughts drum in Beth's mind. Why couldn't Tabitha see it? She wasn't afraid when I told her about the hauntings, because she hasn't experienced anything like that. And yet, those paintings of Harry's, the way she shuts them up, imprisons them, are they not five ghosts she has lived with for nearly as many years? How our conversation has tired and depressed me, and left me feeling very lonely. The worn-out words we both used, her long gaze when she leant over me, the lack of any useful answer . . . Who can help me, after that travesty of friendship? Not Theron. Not Jake. Not Ash. Ash, in my dream, carrying her breasts in a silver dish, with Satan in sun-glasses walking behind her, Ash, with a flower sprouting from her neck-stump, her severed head half-hidden behind the curtain: no, no, I will not think of her.

And Theron does not want his 'life' with Vellet to be disturbed, altered, ended. The rain will not wash his weakness away. And I see the shadow of rain each evening, I feel my own memories sweating blood: how she sucked him, how he panted for the ghost's tongue against him . . .

Beth comes to the abbey ruins. The hill of the Giant rises sharply above her. She walks rapidly through the old graveyard. There are no ghosts here!

There is much to be done, she tells herself, many waiting-rooms to be experienced before I defeat Vellet. But I will defeat her. I will make my name, BETH, stick in her throat and lodged there it will choke her out of being.

Beth is climbing over the stile when a shove from nowhere sends her sprawling and she falls headlong into the hoof-printed mud and muck of the field. A voice laughs, taunting Beth.

'Come on, Beth, join the suicide club. It's a grand life.'

Beth scowls, she is on the blind side of the ghost. She picks herself up, wipes her hands on her raincoat, and stares suspiciously about her but the ruins, the fields and the hillside are empty of people and ghouls. Beth looks ruefully at the mud caked on her shoes and stockings but will not turn back. I will go up to the Giant, she says aloud. And begins to climb the hill. Vellet returns to her own flooded lands, pleased to find Beth so open to her haunting. She will try more tricks with Beth another time.

Seated on her giant's rainy shoulder, Beth feels that she is the sea: carrion and coast, waves and sea-wrack. Above her, the evening sky is a grey groin forced open. I am the sea, thinks Beth, a sea that lives on drownings, of mice, voles, insects, horses, sailors and many crazy women. From her slipshod seat in the wet turf, she cries,

'Giant! Show me my enemy! Show me Vellet, as she was, living. Show me!'

It is a half-moon that slithers between rainclouds, cut in half by Magdalen as she wanders through the pastures. Beth thought she saw the limbs of the Giant move once, whitely, snakily, and then, in place of the white chalk limbs, Beth sees a woman, a young woman holding herself stiffly, determined not to weep. It is Vellet.

Beth holds her breath and watches.

Vellet is speaking. She says to a man Beth does not recognize, 'I am the woman you may kill by inches.' The man does not reply. Perhaps he smelt Vellet's monthly blood. Perhaps he sees her plasma shroud. Vellet flinches from his silence, she moves into the blackness of her own silence in this sordine room. 'Please . . .' she whispers to the man. He turns away and the door closes behind him, leaving Vellet motionless beneath towers of silence on which great birds of mars perched. 'By inches,' she whispers.

'You! Vellet,' mouths Beth.

Out of a night of insects and animals, night of woman, night dividing pain from pain, night thrusting out its raw lips, treeless night in which a man and a woman both stand four miles tall, Vellet wakes to find Theron standing in the doorway, speaking her name, irately. He says to her, 'No, you will always exist, Vellet, you and your kind.' Vellet does not answer. When he'd got what he came for, and left her alone again, she was thirsty. She got up and drank a glass of red wine. The wine tasted of meat. She has an appointment which she fears to keep yet dare not break. She listens at Theron's door and hears him snoring. YES and NO throb in Vellet's head, contradicting her, wounding her. In the addict's garden, Vellet sees a man sitting on the ground, waiting for her. He is the man who will sell her what she wants. What she has to have. YES. NO. YES. NO. YES. NO. Like a drum that man in the garden is beating.

Beth watches the tableau the giant shows her, biting her lip. She remembers that in far places mothers will eat a stillborn child so that the spirit may be reborn through her.

Before Vellet made her decision, to go to the man, to buy what he offered, she saw clowns veiled in red taffeta, she saw rivers flowing too fast, too dark, she saw the locked door, she saw her own key that would unlock that door. The clowns wept and ran away from Vellet.

The man watching the house shifted further back into the shadows. He is the same man who refused to give Vellet the stuff yesterday. Get the money, he insisted.

The side door of the house opens slowly and a woman appears, aphis woman, walking towards the yew tree where he is waiting. Vellet is not weeping, though her hands quiver with the treachery of white seabirds; she needs to score. He spoke to her. 'The money?' he said, not even bothering to colour his words with contempt. She said nothing, smiled slightly, said not one word, moved through the shadows, as if she really were the calm good daughter of the philosopher. She brushed back her hair with a gesture he did not understand, a raindark smile he hated. He looked into her face. He held out his hand for the envelope of banknotes, checked it, sighed as he handed her the package of drugs. She took the parcel in her left hand, she betrayed none of her eagerness, except that her smile twitched almost imperceptibly. 'Be careful,' he said. 'Do not fear,' she said formally, 'I value every grain, you can trust me.'

He watched her slip in through the side door, heard the key turn in the lock, then he moved away through the trees, silently.

Beth is wounded by this vision of Vellet.

'Poor Vellet,' she said, truthfully. Poor Vellet, goes the rain. The scab-skin of night has formed. The wind off the east smells of fish oil. Beth is exhausted by her glimpse of Vellet and is about to trudge downhill, go home with her worries, when she realizes the giant has more to show her. Reluctantly, she settles to watch, pulling the collar of her gaberdine raincoat higher about her neck and hugging her arms around herself for warmth.

In this next vision of Vellet, it is another kind of night, warm, sultry, rainless. Vellet is wandering along the path at the foot of Giant Hill, munching an apple. She seems to be waiting for someone.

Beth waits. In this entangled situation she finds it hard to remember that she is the real girl and Vellet the phantom. She is sure that by the manner in which Vellet is pacing, waiting, that something terrible will happen, branding both of them. Beth dislikes spying on Vellet, especially as the idea of the winged skull of Ash keeps coming to her, with its shadow. But Beth has to see what happens next.

Vellet is still pacing up and down the little path and Beth can smell the jeremiad that moves with her. Vellet throws her apple core away. The soundtrack sighs, the sculpture of a woman on the hillside cries out in loneliness, and there is no exit.

Can it be, Beth wonders, that Theron actually prefers masturbation to me, and that because I am insulted by his preference, I have invented this ghost to deny my responsibility, to camouflage Theron's rejection of me. Is Vellet my poltergeist phenomenon?

Two men are approaching Vellet. They are young men, dressed in leather jackets, jeans, the proper gear. Vellet stands on the path to receive them, greet them. It seems as if she is asking them a question. Then she offers them something from a paper packet. They are eating what she offers, her technicolour host. Vellet and the two young men sit on the grass and talk, laughing, kidding around. Beth cannot hear what they say. She hears only her own blood beating against her eardrums. Vellet, you are the odour of sickrooms, she thinks.

Beth does not want to go on watching. The trio of her vision have such an air of violence about them. They are smoking now, they pass a cigarette from hand to hand.

Beth wants to get up and run away, but she cannot move. The giant says to her: 'I am the wifeless giant, I go back as far as anything can. I will pass my knowledge on, Beth! Stay here. Watch. Learn. You must understand Vellet. Do not be content simply with rejecting her. Think of her as a part of yourself, denied and repressed. Watch Vellet and her two boyfriends, Jo Silverpiece and Vic Coppercoin. Watch her.'

So Beth watches. She watches Vellet, Jo and Vic in their nakedness, their dance between the eyes of the giant. She saw Vellet dancing like a blind ballerina. This is a riddle, thought Beth, and it is not just about a ghost, it is about a woman. It concerns me. Fearfully, she watches. The long pricks of the men joggle as they dance and the mouths of the men are open, their heads thrown back, and their mouths yelling slowly. Vellet dances between the two men, her breasts like two inkblots in the moonlight. She is crouching between the two men now and urinates on the ground. The men are smiling, still dancing, but more slowly. Vellet turns her back on the men, and waggles her arse. First Jo Silverpiece, then Vic Coppercoin kneel down and kiss her arsehole.

Beth's eyes ache and burn. She peers down at the three lovers and tastes the thumbnail of the murdered woman.

Now the men stroke their own erections while Vellet watches, seated on the giant's prick. Her smile is martial, her demeanour vigorous. She watches the men with the red eye of her cunt. She lies on the earth, limbs spread-eagled. The men begin to abuse her.

'No,' said the Giant, correcting Beth, 'no, not abuse. They are only carrying out orders, Vellet's orders.'

Silverpiece has his penis in her mouth. Coppercoin is fucking her. Beth sees Vellet's body quiver and convulse. Coppercoin and Silverpiece change places. Then Coppercoin fucks her in the anus, while Silverpiece winds her hair around his prick.

These sexual acrobatics make Beth's skin burn. She tastes her disgust in her mouth. She feels faint and thinks, God, if this woman's corruption was so strong that she created a ghost for herself, to keep her image abroad in the world after her death, then how can I free Theron of such a wife? Vellet, Vellet, that stink of bowels is you, then!

The antics of the trio continue but Beth closes her eyes and refuses to watch the giant's show any more, so with the palm of his hand he wipes the vision away.

Beth sat on the wet hillside, her flesh stuck full of needles. Now she realizes Vellet's strength. How Vellet's fingers will always reach for the fruit of the tree of voluptuousness. Dirt! thinks Beth. But I have undertaken this work, of ridding Theron of Vellet, even though the work may be beyond my strength. Beth cannot bring herself to stir, even though she is cold and wet.

What happens now, Giant, she thought listlessly.

There is no answer.

The eyelids of Hades close . . .

Beth's sigh is like chalk crumbling in her hand. She still feels sick, cannot get the events she has witnessed out of her mind. How long ago did that orgy take place? How long after that night did Vellet drown? Did Coppercoin or Silverpiece push her in the river, rebelling against her leadership? Beth feels that her own undergarments have been abused. She looks around, almost guiltily. Now Vellet approaches, she cannot smell or sense the ghost's presence, it is the replay of Vellet's adventure that is sickening Beth, and yet at the same time she would like to insert her fingers deep into her own vagina.

I must either help Theron, or leave him.

She shivers violently, cold as if she were standing up to her neck in a stream. Might just as well be, she thinks, and gets up stiffly. Her sweat is beginning to smell rank.

From a long way off, Vellet watches Beth go downhill over the dark grey grass. She sees the broken branches of her own kith and kin. Vellet looks at the man in the moon. Then she whispers, so you showed her, Giant. Why? What are you planning for me? He did not answer her. She sank down in the river again, despairing. Beth's pain is no comfort to her. Beth will be on her guard, now, even stronger an opponent. Vellet cursed, and cats and dogs shuddered in the village. Her open mouth screamed as the Giant chastised her, and the river mud filled her lungs again.

Beth walks briskly to get warm and although she still feels horribly sick, she knows she has been toughened, that the Giant has taught her the use of her eyes, that she knows what she is up against. She has, in fact, been given a shield of defence against Vellet, having seen her at her worst, and she understands that Theron need not feel guilty for her death. Such a woman will inevitably find her death early, violently. It is this guilt of Theron's that Vellet trades on, Beth realizes. If I can remove that guilt, will he be free? Perhaps.

Despite the shocks she's had tonight, and those on top of the frustration of her meeting with Tabitha, Beth feels her sickness ebb away and her spirits rise. After the strain, euphoria. She knows she should not trust it but she does, and she is singing quietly to herself as she comes through the village streets. The odour of beer comforts her as she passes the pub and she is glad to be down among the ordinary houses and the village people. Every lighted window cheers her up and she feels nothing will stop her dealing with Vellet and putting a stop to all this trouble and worry.

Then she crossed the road and saw, in the gutter, a dead black cat, stiff and swollen, a parody cat, a stilted animal waiting for the garbage collector in the morning.

A message from Vellet, thinks Beth, and walks on soberly.

SEVENTEEN

TOWARDS the end of June, Theron asks Beth what she would like for her birthday next week. She frowns, tells him she will go up to town and look around the shops. But she is thinking, secretly, what I want for my birthday is to spend the day at Ash's house, invisible, silent, just overlooking her life. Beth walks quickly away from Theron, so that he will not guess her thought. Her cool response returns Theron to his isolation, to his birdlime ghost.

Beth lifts the lid of the piano and plays a favourite tune, one that always reminds her of rocks and cliffs, of the sea. Her left hand and her right hand move delicately over the keys. She goes on playing, thinking of nothing and no one, her hands imitating shadows.

As I play the music mingles with an odour of slowly decaying fruit in an overripe room. The sullying of fruit amazes me, the malcontent of apples rubs at my groin. Beth jumps up from the piano stool and hurries to the table. She opens the bible with sweaty fingers. She bends over the black blood of the book. She wants to know everything. She would give anything to know . . . But when she tries to read the words the edges of her eyelids feel raw and she is half-blinded with fear.

For the third time in as many hours, Beth unlocks her polished wooden box, bought in the village junk shop, and takes out the six photographs of Ash. Sitting on the edge of her bed, she pores over the snapshots. Beth took them herself with her aunt's old camera that summer five years ago. The smile of Ash is like the roar unidentified in a distance at night, her expressions shift like smoke of that old summer.

Ash, murmurs Beth, poor years since you went with Jake. Nearly five years since I caught the fever of you that still burns me up, even though neither of us are those girls any more, those virgins are no longer us, no more than a soldier's a soldier after he's been demobbed. We're women who never write letters to one another.

Yet my life is still jammed up by this . . . interest I have in you. And you? Are you still running from me? Do you ever think of our summer? Or doesn't it enter your head?

In the room of sporadic sunlight, Beth locks the photographs of Ash away, safe.

Strange name, strange power.

Beth is taking off her clothes.

I am not able to practise the calligraphy of my love for Ash, not even on the walls of public lavatories, that way is not possible for me. I cannot proclaim my love that way. There are always my doubts . . .

But sun and moon maim me, and I keep my right hand prepared for pornographic tasks.

Alpha, Ash, Alpha . . .

Beth shouts silently to the women of Jerusalem.

A child's pink hair ribbon lies on the dusty carpet. Ash stares at it. It is the shape of the lower jaw of a horse. It is the fin of a fish. It is a ribbon, her child's hair ribbon.

In the darkening room, Ash shuts her eyes. The life drains out of her, fluid from a wound. The day, boat of hours, has drifted away from her. This morning, first thing, when she saw the morning mist on the ground, the trees scratching the green sky, she felt she could look into the day and not be afraid of it.

But between her and her existence within the day, her wholeness, have come the heavy weight of other people, their words, gestures, demands: husband, children, friends, the gossip that follows tappings on the door, the thriving of trivia. So Ash's day has gone and now it is twilight, a stone of great size beneath which she is pinned, against which she heaves with no result. And the hours that passed, into which she could not see, could not hold close like flowers or pages to contemplate, those hours are mildewed.

She bends down and picks up the hair ribbon, opens her drawer and drops it in, and is about to close it when she pauses, reaches in the drawer and takes out another ribbon, of black velvet, on which she sometimes fastens a silver medallion depicting a crescent moon. She rummages about in the drawer till she finds the medallion, clasps it in her hand until it gets warm. Then she threads it on to the ribbon and ties it around her neck. Comforted, she goes downstairs.

Last night she had dreamt she was slapping a small child, a little girl, and on waking she thought, but there is no danger. During the day she became certain there was danger, for her.

EIGHTEEN

The Giant in Summer

The giant looks up at the sky.
The giant inhales the innuendoes of the afternoon.
The giant laughs at the idea of an easy death.
The giant outwits god at card games.
The giant wears no loin cloth.
The giant sings of his blindness:
   'the herbage of my eyes'.
The giant breaks the bride's back.
The giant drowns his verdicts in the fountain.
He has no name.
He does not drink blood.
The giant looks at the hour-glass.
The giant plucks his own heart out, gazes at it,
   replaces it, roaring with strength.
The unworldly giant stammers and candles blaze.
The giant speaks the word 'snowdrop' in French:
   'perce-neige'.
The giant listens to a wireless, message that glitters with evil.
The giant watches the apparition, her shimmer.
The giant understands the sleepwalker's language.
He hears the driftwood's mirth.
The giant pricks his finger sewing baby-linen.
The giant smells the sorrel odour of the rain.
The giant meets with thieves and clubs them with his white
   umbrella.
The giant meditates amid the wooden torrents of the afternoon
   on secrets everybody knows.
The giant hires a harlot.
The giant awaits the return of Ash, with mud on her skirt,
   and oak leaves in her womb.
Then he sleeps.
The galactoid gaps in his memory must be repaired.

NINETEEN

BETH turns off the ignition, sits for a moment in the parked car. What will happen after the flowers? she thought, after this pale summer of abandoned orchards? She heaves the two shopping baskets from the back seat and struggles to the door with the week's provisions. She fumbles for the house key, then gets in, dumping the bags on the kitchen table.

Her head aches with the thud and clang of the supermarket. She always goes once a week but wonders whether the double stamps are worth the ordeal of crowds, ill-tempered women and bawling children. A village of shoplifters, anyway, she thought bitterly.

Beth lit a cigarette and sprawled in the fireside chair, though there is no fire in the grate. It is July, although the weather is dull as secondhand clothes. She draws the smoke deep into her lungs. For the past fortnight she's been sleeping badly and her body feels fussy, disorganized, her strength going, everything changing, her own face like that of a different woman reflected intermittently in mirrors and windows.

I've scratched myself on Theron's barbed wire cock, she thinks.

I held your hand, Theron, last evening as we stood at the foot of the stairs. I held your hand, you clutched my fingers, you said, 'I'm afraid, Beth,' with your head you made the gesture 'no', and I saw her falling towards us down the stairs in a shadow, passing us like a chill breeze, and you clutched my hand, hurting my fingers, you shuddered: and Vellet's ghost left behind her a hard auriferous sensation that parted us yet again and Theron and I began to run away from one another in this house. It is no laughing matter, we ran all night, our words so unkind, so cruel, we ran with our quarrel, our rage burning us like the edge of a moon, and we could not stop, not until I screamed and shrieked and hooted with hysteria, a real attack, no rumour, and you saw that it was me, Beth, me and not Vellet: you saw the danger of your mirage. We calmed down, we were both shivering, sweating. I pushed the hair back from my face, got up from the bed, naked, and staggered under the shower, warm water on my face, tits, ankles. 'I'm not afraid now,' you called out. I nodded, exhausted. 'She won't visit again tonight,' he said confidently, when I came out of the shower. I was so tired, and wounded from the fight. The silence moved between us again. I stuck my tongue out at it. You laughed, Theron, and hope revived in me, that you might free yourself of Vellet, shuck her off.

But can I trust to that? My mind turns more often to my own house, safe escape, high up on the moors. My house, untenanted, unhaunted. Vellet will not follow me there. It is Theron she wants. I am coming closer and closer to the break, I feel it, I know that one day, in the dark time before dawn, I shall creep out of this haunted house where there is not enough room for two wives. Vellet will have won. As I leave I'll laugh without making a sound for my head will be full enough of noises. Poor Theron. I shall leave you and be free of the mewing of Vellet, free of the ghost swimming towards me in the naked night.

Often, Theron appears to enjoy his ghost. Oh he protests to me, no, Beth, I do not enjoy it. But she has a hold over me (he says) and somehow, it is as if, when she is here, I don't care what she does or how she does it. I said to him, 'you're welcome, Theron, go ahead, have your fun.'

He said then, 'Beth, I understand your angry words, I know how you feel, squeezed into a tiny lonely jealous room.'

'Do you,' I said.

Last night, the moon turned aside when I looked up at the sky.

Last night, when we were hoarse with our dispute, I put out my hand and scratched his cheek with my long nails, drawing blood.

Later, in bed, I was almost asleep when I felt you shift, Theron, move, your touch on my shoulder, and then the weight of your body, coming down on mine. You were excited and you caressed me without satire. Without speech, no explanation, no word, you touched my thigh and then to acknowledge a reconciliation you fingered my cunt. Last night was the first time we'd had sex for weeks.

Beth stubs out her cigarette, begins the tedious chore of unpacking groceries, the eggs, butter, bacon, flour, bread, apples, oranges, coffee, raw meat.

She opens the larder door and smells the cold summer in there too.

All the while her thoughts are creasing and wrinkling and she feels she is moving rapidly away from any solution. There is no cure for me and Theron. Nothing to salvage from what might have been a shared life. Vellet is a gag thrust into my mouth. I have only silence and retching left to me.

He gets strength from Vellet, even though he says he hates and fears her. Perhaps they are operating a two-way vampirism, sustaining one another. Where does that leave me?

Beth is almost weeping but will not give in, pulls herself together. Putting the kettle on to boil, she glances through the kitchen window at a miserable sky with bits of blue the size of midges. I feel I've lived as long as the giant, she thinks.

Theron fingered my cunt as calmly as if he didn't have two wives. I felt the pummel of his cock against my buttocks. He weaved his touch restlessly but delicately. After his encounters with Vellet, I didn't want him to fuck me, but the weeks of chastity had been too long, left my body unwieldy, so I didn't push him away, I couldn't, I gasped, he was trying to catch fish in my nets, I was fresh from the furnace, he was groaning above me and I was panting and swearing, heaving myself up to the many-seeded man, my throat marked with red blotches, and sinuous flames darting up my spine: yes, we sped on our way, hearts banging loud in our ears.

Beth sips her tea.

Now I am disgusted with myself, she thinks, exactly because I am not ashamed of what happened last night, that consummation. I should be, but I am not. I know he's turned on by the ghost of his first wife, and is slaking himself on me. But I wanted it. I should be revolted by that, but I'm not. I just don't know how long I can go on with this strange tension. I ought to clear out, go back to my own home. My love is being clipped, my branches lopped off. To make me grow straighter? I don't know. If I go, am I running away? If I stay, will I grow straight, or crooked and crazy?

Beth strikes her hand repeatedly against her hip. What am I to do?

The phone rang. She jumped up.

'Yes?'
'It's me, Beth.'
'Hello, Theron.'
'You know that bookcase just by my desk?'
'Yes.'
'On the top shelf, you'll find my annotated copy of Bullock's Hitler. I left it behind this morning. Can you bring it in to the university for me, dear? Before three this afternoon? Does that upset your day?'
'No, Theron, no. I'd enjoy the drive anyway.'
'Fine. See you about two thirty?'
'Sure.'
She put the black receiver back on its cradle gently, then ran upstairs and brushed her hair vigorously. Then she made the beds, cleaned the bathroom, came downstairs again, got the hoover out of the broom cupboard, cleaned the house while her thoughts piled up like dirty dishes in the sink.

And out of all Beth's confusion, what? No decision, no way out discovered, no exit from her embattled area. These are the quicksands of Uranus, she thinks, as she parks her car in the university yard. For me, there's little difference now between singing and screaming. I must get free before it's too late.

She left the book with Theron's secretary, he was busy in a tutorial session. The secretary wanted to talk, glad of an excuse, but Beth did not stay, she was trussed up in the same ghostly inflorescence that had been hers all day. She drove out of the town and along a narrow road between fields. She feels her mind stretched across regions of brilliant metal, with no place to rest.

How can Theron go on with his lectures, his krieg-talk to the students, sit and discuss old battles and strategies, when his own life is so jagged, war-like, his world tightening around him, invading him. But perhaps he does not notice the danger. I come back again to the same question. Should I leave him? Because he is happy with his ghost wife. Let him have his formal masturbator's life. Let him look deeply into the eyes of the ghost. The impeccable mouth of the ghost!

Beth drew into a lay-by and got out of the car. At least I am out of the house, away from those silent rooms with their slavonic clocks. Perhaps one day of some sort, the day after tomorrow, or one day next month, a warmer day, the door will unlock, this door I'm facing, this door I'm hammering against, and it will swing open easily on the prospect of glittering lakes and fountains, and I, one day, without warning, will be invited to that country, and Ash, you'll step forward, and lead me into that place.

Beth crosses the road and walks across a field. On the other side of the century, my life stretches out freely, with flowers and friends, days the colour of wheat, not these pale chill days. The wind drags her thoughts through the grass. She looks up at the giant. He is three miles walk away. She sees him preening his whiteness.

'What are your habits, giant? Do you catch fish by poisoning the waters with your own urine? Do you live on bones, nerves and embryos? What are the names of your daughters?'

'These are the names of my daughters,' said the giant, his breath billowing like dry ice.

> 'My daughters are called Amulet, Ash, Ararat,
> Beauty, Beulah, Breast,
> Cunt, Coffin, Crown,
> Dog, Dream and Dust,
> Eve, East and Egg,
> Fish, Flamen and Famine,
> Gospel, Grace and Glass,
> Hallow, Hag and Husk,
> Iron, Itch and Island,
> January, Juniper and Jackdaw,
> Kerosene, Kaleidoscope and Kale,
> Lamp, Luck and Lapwing,
> Moth, Map and Mask,
> Net, Newt and Night,
> Oak, Orgasm and Ouija,
> Palfrey, Prairie and Plough,
> Question, Quilt and Quartz,
> Rubble, Ring and Rain,
> Shadow, Shore and Shrapnel,
> Tree and Turtle and Twilight,

Udder and Umber and Uterus,
Vagina and Vampire and Veil,
Waltz and Wave and Wimple,
Xanthin and Xenolith and Xylophone,
Yew and Year and Yoni,
Zodiac and Zona-Pellucida and Zephyr.
These are the names of my daughters, Beth.'

Beth goes on looking at the rough bluish sky behind the giant. The giant's erection turns Beth's clothes to tatters. The wind flaps the remains of her skirt around her legs.

'How many wives have you, giant?' she whispers, her mouth dry.

'None,' he answers softly. 'None.'

Now Beth feels herself plunge headlong into her own womb.

'Vellet? Is she not a daughter of yours?'

'No,' he answers. 'She is no daughter of mine. She is no one's daughter.'

His voice is laborious now, his blind eyes pits of chalk.

'How many sons have you, giant?'

'No sons,' he says, 'I have no sons.'

'And tell me,' asks Beth fearfully, 'What is the name of my daughter?'

The giant does not answer Beth's question. There is only silence, and the wind moving across the field, down from the hills. Beth stares at the giant cut into the chalk hill. Then she begins to move cautiously back to her car, her flesh creaking with random guesses. And the lining of her womb is woven so as to change colour, according to the time of night or day.

Singing or screaming a lunar song?

Beth cannot distinguish between the two modes. She moves stealthily. She stands at the gate of her own house. The moorland is cold and quiet around her. 'Where was the tree?' she sings. 'In a garden,' she croons.

In the porch of the house there are snuffling shadows. The red paint is peeling from the front door. Beth turns the key in the lock.

It is stiff, she exerts pressure, hurting her fingers, but the resistance gives, and the door opens.

Beth pauses on the threshold of her house, the names of the Giant's daughters reverberating in her mind. Why do those names remind me of the little pearly birthmark on Ash's left cheekbone, that splash of moon?

On the doorstep, Beth hesitates, afraid of the dusty loneliness inside the house, petrified of the mirrors that once reflected Ash.

The sky shudders with the irritation of a botched summer. The overgrown garden murmurs retarded proverbs. With a surly smile Beth enters her house, re-enters the sheeted rooms of her adolescence. In the house she discovers a leviathan stillness. All is muffled, stifled.

How long has it been? thinks Beth. Over a year since I've been inside this house. Usually I peer in through the windows, just staying in the garden. This house has been empty too long. It's become sad, sadder than when I left. My house is uncared for . . . it should be lived in, made alive. Shall I run out of the house before something catches me? I can if I want to . . . No voice will call me back, no ghost detain me.

Beth pulls the front door to, shutting herself in. The hall is dark. The house smells damp.

Slowly she climbs the stairs and goes into the little lavatory built into the alcove at the turn of the stairs. She pulls down her pants and urinates. Then she tries to shit but finds it is only wind stretching her bowels.

How can Ash be one of the Giant's daughters?

I don't know.

She glances out of the lavatory window, down at the old greenhouse, and beyond that, the yard in which they used to keep chickens.

Beth pulls the chain.

My body aches, thinks Beth, as if I were a sword-swallower, an inexperienced one, a novice. She is at the top of the stairs. Her movements are slow. She opens the doors of the bedrooms, as if unlocking a harem. The bare iron frames of the beds are harsh and ugly in the thin light. Heavy wardrobes loom. Beth opens the windows. The chill air comes in, butting against the dirty curtains.

Beth holds her own invisible afterbirth in her hand.

She puts her head out of the window and yells,

'Howdy, Vic Coppercoin! Welcome, Jo Silverpiece! Where are you, Vellet?'

Her voice goes palsied through all the neglected rooms, across the coarse garden, but there is no answer. None of the guests accept Beth's invitation. Beth's challenge goes unanswered.

'There! I knew your real name was Mr Blindmaker, Giant,' Beth grumbles. Leap years and lunar years, white languages and black: all yours, Giant, and you can keep them. What did planchette say to me, years ago, in this room? Ash insisted on calling up planchette, though I told her I was scared. It was a hot evening, we'd been drinking vodka, drinking pretty heavily. Four times Ash received a message and each time all planchette said was, go away, Beth, go away, Beth, go away, Beth, go away, Beth.

Planchette's command or Ash's desire?

I went out of the room that night, I tiptoed out of our room and along this corridor, listening to the sounds of my body. That night the clock rode naked until dawn. But that was a long time ago.

Another night, not in the same room, but downstairs, on a calm unelaborate summer night, with the french windows thrown wide open and a moon with its roots in us and stars like steppingstones: on that ghostless night I sat at the piano and Ash sang. Her song was called *A Secret Understanding* and the words made us both blush. Later that night Ash unplaited my hair with her long fingers. That night I wandered out of my cage and (because the puppet wanted to be human!) went to Ash. Female bears with honey on their paws. It was a long time ago. Another night we washed our feet in clear river water. Even now when I think of Ash, explosions of an unknown but terrifying nature go through me.

How can she be a daughter of the giant?

One night shortly after Jake's arrival, he and I went out for a walk. It was dark and moonless so Jake brought a torch with him. In fact, Ash suggested he take the torch, so that we didn't stumble in the dark.

'How have you been, Beth?' he asked, after we had been walking some time.

'Great!' I answered expressionlessly, 'no wars, no floods destroyed me.'

It was a warm autumn night but iron hooks clipped the stars to the sky. I shivered, smelling Jake's strength, sensing his intentions. We walked in silence by the pond. The trees by the waterside were old and hard and I knew they had voices and they could speak and when they did what they said would be terrible. Jake walked faster and then turned, asking,

'Are you happy, Beth?'

I couldn't answer him.

'Are you?' he repeated, making me look at him, shining the torch full on my face. He was not angry, he spoke quietly, but I knew I had to answer him, I knew it, even if we had to stay there until dawn and its billowing smoke. How well I remembered his gestures from our childhood, the wrench of his mouth, the narrowing of his eyes, his head and hand and heel, the stranger he'd grown up into. I remembered one day in particular when we were children, his clothes spattered with red paint, and how he teased me, dabbing me with the wet paint brush until I cried.

'Are you happy?' he repeated, softly.

'I was,' I told him. 'Yes,' I whispered, 'I was.'

'Before I came?'

'Yes.'

'When you and Ash were alone?'

'Yes.'

When Jake smiled, there was a darkness at all hours of the clock. He pointed the torch towards the pond and flicked a beam of light this way and that carelessly across the water.

'But you know it can't go on . . . don't you?' he said, almost lightly.

I said nothing.

'You realize how crazy it is, you two girls?' He laughed. How did I feel then, knowing he despised me and that he would take Ash away? I felt I was the rain, the dirt, a nun's shadow, no more.

'Do you understand, Beth?' he asked sharply, his grip tightening around my forearm.

'She must decide,' I said weakly.

He relaxed his grip.

'Why, yes, that's fair, surely,' he said, grinning, 'we'll let Ash choose.'

I nodded my head.

'That is fair, isn't it?' he asked a minute later, in a sing-song voice. I nodded again. I did not want to be Beth any more.

We leaned on the fence and stared through the darkness across the moor. Jake lit a cigarette and the escarpment of smoke hurt my eyes. There was a dog barking somewhere far off, and the sheep moved in the darkness. I was the only casualty in the night. All of this was years ago, though.

Beth, the coprophagan, stands again at the edge of the pond. It is the present now, not the past. Her conversation with Jake, years past, echoes and fades. Her body feels luminous. She must not linger in the twilight much longer. The rain begins, whisper of latinisms. Beth will sell her body very cheaply this evening. Where are the customers, the soldiers, the sailors? She ran out of the old playroom because the old black-faced goggle-eyed fantastically-garbed toy lying on the windowsill frightened her. But even so she might have to return to this house to live soon, leaving Theron, carrying coldness in her hands, to keep night-vigils among the hanks of dream.

Ash wails in darkness, callously. She will not offer Beth any of her uneasy lullabies. Beth must creep back into her own shadowy regions alone, accepting her own penury.

Theron and I cannot answer the important questions we have both posed, therefore I think our dialogue must dissolve. We must take our questions elsewhere. Beth stares over the pond towards the fog of long grass; beyond that, the moorland. She bites the jagged fingernail of her left forefinger. The back of her thighs ache with tension. She looks up at the sky where the greeny light reminds her of someone rubbing glass with a scrap of silk. Beth's heavy hair is bound in two long plaits, reaching almost to her waist, and its weight is increasing, it seems hardly possible that she'll be able to get her body moving again, she is taking root here by the water. The broken thoughts of exhaustion confuse her, and it seems as if her mother's silhouette is reflected in the grey waters of the pond. Beth gasps, touches her sweating forehead with her thin hand.

'Your fires and lamps are to be extinguished,' said Jake, that night he told me he and Ash were to be married. Ash had gone up to bed but Jake and I still sat talking, the empty bottles of wine littering the table. Then he cut the cards and said, 'do you want to know your fortune?' He smiled covetously. 'Tell me,' I said. He moved his hands rapidly over the pasteboards. 'It is never new enough for you, Beth,' he said, 'the new year, the new moon: beware, Beth. The man you'll marry will live up a one-way street, sensual but too silent.'

That night Jake told me ancient jokes.

'I have had many wives in many languages,' he boasted.

'All obese, I bet,' I answered.

He snorted with laughter. I survived until the next page. But he took Ash and left me with a body that looks like that of a young woman but to me resembles the body of a dismantled ship, unwieldy, unseaworthy.

Crossing the lawn, Beth sees the triangle of dancers standing still, too late to begin dancing, Ash, Beth, Jake.

Beth hurries through the garden.

My brains are in my arsehole, my womb is kept in a polythene bag stored under my bed, she thinks feverishly. All that I had has gone, is different, and I hear the calendar combing her hair.

Vellet does not haunt me here. She has no need. I have my own ghosts here, to whom I am addicted. In my dream last night Jake called up the baby-bat hurricane. Jake lifted the jugs one by one, filling them with September cider. 'Do I make you afraid?' he asked me fiercely. I did not answer. I saw Ash in the background, opening an iron cupboard. She was dressed in a military uniform of some kind.

I've had enough of these reminiscences. I'll go back to Theron, to try a little longer, before the sacred bone of my pelvis wears out with trying. I'll leave my house, this dangerous refuge, with its half-healed wounds, and go back to Theron's world.

His world: the puzzle, the charade of the stallion's shadow, the place where night begins.

Beth and Theron are reading. On the radio, a music perseveres. Outside, the rain is taken for granted. A moon is drizzling down also.

Theron exclaimed suddenly and looked up.

'Beth,' he said excited, 'Beth . . .'

'What?' she said, not looking up, absorbed in her detective novel.

'Do you know what the first vertebra in the human neck is called?'

Beth stared at him.

'What a strange question, Theron. No, what is it called?'

'Atlas!'

Beth looks bewildered and glances around the room, as if the ghost might enlighten her as to the significance of the vertebra called Atlas. But this is the ghost's night off.

'I don't understand, dear,' she said.

'But don't you? I meant how poetic the names of the various regions of the body are, unsuspected, hidden beneath the skin. The first vertebra, Beth, that holds up the neck, called Atlas, because Atlas held up the world. His figure is often put on the title-pages of atlases to this day. And the vertebra supports the world of the head.'

'Ah, I see now. Yes, that is very neat, very exact, Theron.'

'I thought so,' said Theron, pleased, and smiling at Beth. She looks a little tired, he thinks. He goes back to his book, but only a few moments later interrupts their reading again.

'By the way, isn't it strange we never hear from Ash and Jake now? You never hear from Ash nowadays, do you?'

Beth's wrists and ankles ache. But she does not look up from her book.

'No,' she says abstractedly, 'no. I had a few letters soon after she and Jake married, but not now. She's busy. With a young family, you can't expect . . . why do you ask?'

'It seems strange to me . . . your own family never in touch.'

'We were never close, you know that.'

'He and Ash might have died, for all we know.'

Beth shrugged, felt sick.

'So you didn't get on? You and Jake?'

Beth threw down her book. Theron ignored her gesture.

'No, we didn't get on.'

'And Ash?'

Beth hesitates, watching Theron. He is only gossiping.

'I hardly knew Ash,' said Beth quietly.
'I thought she lived with you?'

Beth got up and walked to the window, pulled the curtain aside, peered out at the rainy evening. What is Theron's reason for this conversation, what is he hinting at? Or is he only passing time, tired of his book, of the idea of Atlas?

'She lived with me just a few weeks during the summer of the year she married Jake, she met him while she was staying with me. It was lonely for me, you know, up there in that big house, so isolated, not a neighbour for miles. Ash didn't pay any rent but she helped out with shopping, cleaning, instead. When Jake came home, he and Ash hit it off.'

'So you were a matchmaker,' said Theron, laughing. Beth turns on him sharply, but his laughter is innocent enough.

'As you say, I was. And it is strange that we never hear from them.' Beth sighs, sits down again, takes up her book.

Then Theron says insolently,

'Had quite a fancy for Ash, didn't you?' The silence splits into two equal halves. In one half, Theron waits for an answer. In the other, Beth struggles for breath. No ferries cross the cold river between Beth and Theron. Beth is sure that her skinny body is emitting an offensive odour.

'Bastard!' she whispers, digging her nails into the palms of her hands.

He heard her.

'I'm not the only one with a secret then, am I?' he said angrily.

'Did I say you were?' she replied.

'You didn't tell me about Ash. You implied that you were perfect. You left me to be the shitty one.'

Beth threw herself back in her chair and slashed with the blades of her hands through the air. Her skin is metallic, she does not recognize the abuse she is mouthing.

He got up without a word and beckoned to his wife.

Beth hesitated, then stood up, a culprit, uttering light rapid incoherent sounds. She followed him upstairs and into their bedroom.

Unhurriedly, he smeared a clear cold ointment on her bum, his kind of witch's ointment.

TWENTY

ASH is hunched over her sewing but keeps glancing up out of the window at the shortcoming of the grey sky. She is menstruating and she is gloomy. Her shadow bites the unfinished dress and her hands are penetrated by the sharp points of her thoughts. Her embroideries anger her. Also there are the old spellings she cannot erase from her mind. A slender blind red snake moves in her wet place, nipping her.

I used to visualize my great grandson's life, shining in a cat's cradle mirror, the face of the future. This vision used to sustain me through bad times. Now I do not care about the generations.

Jake is pursuing me. That is the manner of our marriage. I cry superstitiously. He runs after me. My many escapes exhaust me. I am holding my bruised hands out in front of me as I run, to brush aside the leaves that threaten to hit me in the face. I run but hesitate suddenly, cannot decide which path to take. I cannot elude my pursuer, I hear him close behind me. He is chasing me. My son and my daughter are chasing me. The percussion of their voices tortures me.

I am caught.

He will not let me escape.

Bride-harlot, he called me.

Now I ache all over, I clench my muscles tight as one of god's smiles, I throw my sewing down. The afternoon says to me, why aren't you running, Ash, home to the giant.

I gasp and hold my hands over my ears.

Who will write a requiem for me, if I leave Jake? He will follow me.

My other head sprouts, laughs, has its own dreams, eats roots and skins of fruit, plants tomorrow's starvation. As I look at myself in the mirror, I see my hair turn to leaves, my hand is a branch, my cry is mud. I spread my name upon the wounds of Christ.

Last night I stood beside Jake, motionless. He frowned. He took hold of my skirt in both his hands, wrenched and tore the fabric, asked me questions.

'Why do you want to go back there? Is it just sentiment? Why do you want to go back, to the village of the giant?'

I shook my head, tired of all this.

'Why don't you answer me?' he shouted. Then he forced an entry into my trance. His thumbs pressed against my throat. I crawled away from him, a broken woman. I saw in my mind's eye Beth weeping blood as she got out of the train and came towards me. Her hair was blue as the sea. She soaked me in her embrace. I'll teach you star-archery, Ash, she promised. Moons of Europa fell on us.

Now leaf-shadows ache on the afternoon wall. A leaf-ghost trembles against the white door.

Ash unlocks the door of a cupboard and takes out a wicker basket, similar to a picnic hamper. She places it on the table and stands looking at it, her expression taking on a severe radiance.

She lifts the lid of the basket, which gives off a strawy creaking. She takes a deep breath. Inside the basket, a jumble of old pages, old notebooks, coffee-stains on the covers, diaries whose pages she never completed, all the stories of adolescence unfinished, only half told, postcards of cathedral towns, overthrown republics, long dead movie stars. Letters from Jake when he'd been overseas. Ash dabbles her hands through the mementoes. She's never had the courage to burn these memories.

Now she will confront them.

Methodically, she begins to sort the papers. There are forgotten things here for her to rediscover, versions of herself come to light again this afternoon. It is almost unbearable, this thinking back, looking back across wind-beaten years, but her life demands it, and it is harder to turn away from the task now than to complete it.

She reads the poems she wrote long ago in the city, and then the other poems composed in the houses of strangers: the misshapen stanzas remind her that she is a woman now, established, respectable, the mother of children, having a place in the world. It is a long time since she was a girl working in a cheap fish restaurant. But her pride in her position does not last. My unhappiness is not to be washed away like that. Difficult lessons take the longest to be learnt.

She stacks the poems neatly in a pile. How thin my handwriting was then!

She picks up several letters that she wrote to Jake, when he was away in Madrid last summer. She'd never posted them, despite the hours they'd taken her to write, the nights they kept her from sleeping, with the things she wanted to say to him, how they were full of her unhappiness with Jake, yet how she depended on him, loved him. Ruefully she turns the sealed stamped envelopes back and forth in her hands, but cannot bear to open and read her messages. It was very bad then, my depression. I have gone on from that, I see clearer now.

But Ash knows she will never be free of her own silence, her undelivered messages. She feels she is made of mirrors.

Then she smiles light-heartedly. Here are the photographs. Alison, her first child, and James, born a year later; many photographs, from babyhood to first day at playschool. Ash lingers over the photographs with the skin feeling of her babies creeping warmly over her body.

Then suddenly she is very cold. Her tender smile grimaces.

This is not a photograph of children.

This is a photograph of the two girls, untidy, innocent as alphabets. Beth and Ash, arms linked, laughing into the camera held gingerly by Tabitha Irons.

This photograph is like an alarm clock set to awaken Ash from her long sleep, when the moment is ripe.

But why should I suddenly find myself thinking of Beth, drawn back to her? I haven't thought of her for years. Why does the photo of me and Beth shock me, feel like a signal?

Slowly Ash packs the papers, including the last snapshot, into the basket again, locking it away in the cupboard. She is growing angry. The pendulum of her blood swings. Beth and Jake are the same creature: they are both pursuers. Leave me alone, both of you!

She reaches down a book from the shelf, taking one at random, and opening it to read a poem about a woman descending a flight of old steps down to the sea.

Futures were still wailing in her when Jake pushed the door open to see his wife seated at her table, immobile, desolate and dumb.

His heart sank.

'What is it?' he asks anxiously, setting down the cup of tea he has brought her. He looks at the book lying on the floor, spine broken from the violence with which it has been thrown down. He stoops, picks it up, sets it on the table, beside the cup.

Ash looks up at Jake and laughs, hard and humourless. 'Happy Anniversary,' she cries, quoting from the inscription written on the flyleaf of the book, and then rushes out of the room, leaving Jake to pick up the book again, which she has flung away from her.

About what did you dream last night, Ash? thought Jake. And why are the sunlit streets of the early afternoon so desolate to you? They always have seemed so, you told me. Why does it seem to you that our children play doomed games? This is all part of the riddle called Ash. I preferred the period she had last month, she was calm, if deformed, sad among her spiders. There was not this fury.

Jake is groping for a door in the dark. He loves Ash. He has loved her since their first meeting in Beth's garden. He frowns at the thought of Beth. Beth, always resisting him, jealous of the adopted boy, always turning down his friendship. But he'd got Ash. His love is bearing down on Ash more and more each day. She feels the black-gloved hand on her shoulder, beneath which she must bow. His army defeats her, an army made of two children. Yet Jake loves her. And she knows it. It is what shames her, what splutters in her mind like a burning sea-coal. It is what keeps her here, it is what prevents her considering what she would rather have, in place of her accustomed life.

Ash walks in the garden, through the wastes of summer. Her thoughts are illegal activities. She knows that Jake is standing at the window of her room, sipping a cup of tea, watching. In pursuit again.

She will not look up at the window, not wave to him.

She walks by the roses that recoil from her and each other in the windy sunlight.

Why does the recollection of Beth rise up in me now, as from some unsuspected dark place in me? Why does the thought of that long past summer nag me now, why do I feel that in leaving Beth I took a wrong turning? These thoughts are new and strange. I do not want them but perhaps I have nothing else. Why now do I feel the pain of separation? Why not earlier? It was the newness, the excitement. To be married, to have my own house, and then the children, like confirmations of myself, assurances of my own existence. Now that spell is wearing off, and what is left? What is to be done now?

Do I have to go back to the village of the giant?

Always I feared the giant, his white outline dominating the hill, the countryside around; giant, priapic moon-man. I don't want to go back to his domain. But Beth is there, and the end of the story that began for us is there. How afraid I am to go back, to climb Giant Hill and hear what he has to tell me, what I always refused to hear. What will spawn in me then?

Isn't Jake right when he tells me I should be content here? That I have all I need. Yes, he is right. But I cannot curb the sense that a vital element has been left out.

I was content with my placid life, suckling children, taking care of the house, walking dogs, playing with the children, reading and sewing in the evening, sometimes visits to cinemas or theatres with Jake, yoga at the technical college. But this past year my content has worn out. Is it because the children are older, and take less of my time, leaving me alone too much? I looked forward to some peace, as the kids got bigger. But it's not working out like that. I am discontented and Jake merely defers a punishment that might shatter me.

Shall I have another child? Would that put me in a stronger position, regarding Jake? No. He wants me to be pregnant, sees me safest in that condition, and the advantage to me would be only temporary. My womb has done its work. It has grown its creatures.

Why do I want to see Beth again, want to talk to her, ask her advice? I want her as my friend, no more. Years ago, I hated Beth. Beth, who made no effort to keep me out of Jake's custody, who put up no fight, but let him over-rule us both. Beth, whose betrayal made me think I hated her until now. Beth, who I've hated and forgotten. I turned to Jake and found strength in him that delighted me but now scares me.

Whichever way I turn, I cannot spring back into fresh life, I only remain hurt, as one who is hunted can only be hurt.

If I run to the giant, what then?

Her husband's shadow approached, fell over her.

'You do not know me,' she told him scornfully, not turning to him.

He sat down beside her, beneath the limetree and spoke to her quietly until he had swept her clean of her fiery-redness, until he had dissolved that war-dance. She is no longer sinewy. She is meek, she floats like a kite and he holds the string.

TWENTY ONE

AFTER weeks of cloud and the grey summer growing taller and thinner, the weather clears. The sun brightens the paths and linden shadows with its pendulous yellow.

Early in the morning, Beth is pinning up washing to dry. She is wearing a light summer dress, the green material patterned with small white flowers. The sun soothes her, enables her to act without thinking. It gives her a natural body. The damp garments hang motionless on the line.

Beth picks up the empty laundry basket. Since the arrival of the sunlight, she has forgotten the cold stories and the torn marriage map. When she woke to see the sunlight streaming through the curtains, she took a deep breath of relief, as if she'd received a royal pardon. She got up quickly and showered, noting that the soreness in her anus had eased. Alone in the sunny rooms she busied herself happily with various tasks and now strolls by the moist cobwebs of the early garden.

But when Theron awoke in his sunny room, he looked out of the window and saw Vellet. She is holding what seems to be a fan and she is looking upwards as if in fear.

Like a sleepwalker on the motorway, Theron moves around his room. Unlike Beth, he is not changed by the new weather, sunlight does not lighten his load. Vellet smiles at him from the front page of yesterday's newspaper. Theron jerks away from her tabloid grimace only to meet another of her reflections in the sunny mirrors: she is swallowing gold coins and pearls, and laughing. Theron raises his fist to punch the mirror-ghost but now there are only reflections of branches in the mirror, an image of the calm garden's sunlit trees. Theron feels a pulpiness behind his eyes. This is Vellet's first visit for three days.

'Why have you come back?' he asks, smelling the damp address of the ghost.

Vellet sits on the edge of his bed. She murmurs: 'captivity . . .'

'What do you mean, captivity? Mine, or yours?' asks the haunted man unhappily.

'I do not want to be a ghost,' says Vellet. 'To be a soft mean vagrant. I do not want to whine for a touch of love that cannot come to me.'

Theron watches his first wife from his position in the sunlight. Vellet sits in shadows, a spider-tamer.

'Every moment is a lucky-dip tub for me, Theron, and when I thrust my hands in among the shavings all I bring out are booby prizes.'

She falls silent amid the rubble of her death.

'I'm sorry,' says Theron gently.

She nods.

'Your picture, as it seemed to be, in the paper, frightened me, Vellet.'

The ghost of a smile touches Vellet's face.

'Yes,' she agrees, 'I know. But you realize, of course, Theron, that I have permission to haunt you.'

'From whom?'

'Why, from you. If you tell me I must go away, then I will. You will give me no choice. I'll go away and I will not return. If you tell me strongly, honestly. Otherwise, it will not work. And being dead I can recognize your lies. It is you who call me, demand to be haunted.'

Theron shifts in his chair.

'Yes, I have feared as much.'

'Am I to go? Will you let me go, Theron? I too want to be free, not to be this sickly waltzer between light and dark. Let me go!'

The ghost looks up at him eagerly.

But he is silent, shakes his head. Vellet slumps back into the shadows, disappointed.

'I see that my attractions still call you,' she says bitterly, 'that you cannot resist me, that I am still bound to you. It is a defect in us both.'

Theron begins, 'look, Vellet, I want . . .' But she has gone. Theron moves swiftly to the window and peers down into the sun-lit garden. In the early morning he sees Vellet culling dew from the rosebushes to rinse the blood from her sandals. He unlatched the window, leaned out and cried, 'Vellet!'

Beth comes forward, squinting up at him, then smiling.

'What did you say, dear?' she asks pleasantly.

'I only wondered, is breakfast nearly ready?' Beth nods. Out of the corner of his eye, Theron sees Vellet skipping away through the orchard, handcuffed to haunting. He closed the window. As he walked downstairs, he thought of himself as an amputee, still feeling the phantom limb, Vellet. He is anxious to get to the university and to his work, where Vellet rarely disturbs him, because, no doubt, he does not have the leisure to conjure her.

At breakfast, Beth tries to say something important to Theron, but he is abstracted, his attention elsewhere. She wants to say how sorry she is for not telling him about Ash, to tell him he was right to be angry and that she bears him no malice. Beth feels that with the coming of sunlight she has fresh hope that they might both work their troubles out. But when she begins, 'Theron, I am sorry I didn't say about Ash and explain . . .' he interrupts, reproaching her for having brought the subject up. '. . . so let's forget about it, shall we?' he says shortly.

Foliage of the succubus, thought Beth penetratingly, but said nothing. After breakfast, she went to the lavatory and emptied her bowels.

Behind the mirrors, Vellet laughs at the pair of them. She is the shitless ghost. She polishes the giant's halo. She laughs at Beth and Theron. She laughs at herself, a laughter springing from a gross pain.

Theron kisses Beth goodbye, like a miser, and then hurries out to the garage.

Beth stands by the garden gate, waving to him. The car disappears in clouds of dust, turning down the track. Beth's backward grammar did not reach Theron. She wanders from the gate across the lawn to the rustic summerhouse and sits inside, twirling her thumbs.

'Is your back breaking, dear?' asks Vellet. The ghost is sitting beside Beth, shading her watery eyes against the sunlight. The false black birth of the ghost hurts Beth. Her throat, her cunt ache. Ash is tiny and lost in the distance while Vellet brings her ugly song very close.

'Is it you then?' Beth says coldly, 'why don't you go away, Vellet?'

'Tell your husband to send me away,' said Vellet archly, and vanished.

'That would be the answer,' murmured Beth.

Scarlet, the folds of my vagina, she thought. The sun hesitates on the lawn, then grows stronger, and Beth responds again to the opening of the air. The brown birds flit in the garden, from branch to bush. Scents of flowers rise and drift. Amid all the disturbance of her life, Beth does not cling to uglinesses. Theron's angers, lack of sympathy, his slow speech and his dedication to the ghost ... Beth sets herself free from them. She will release herself from him when she comes to the last of her strength. It will be soon, if Theron does not dismiss Vellet.

It is the garden that concerns Beth now, the green and the gold, the unviolated enclosure of flowers, of flaming light and flushed shadows, this is where Beth is at home. She is keenly aware of the late burgeoning of summer and she loves its voluptuousness. She feels the patina of leaves against her skin.

Last night, shortly before midnight, as Beth was preparing for bed, she'd glanced out of the window, expecting to see the full moon, its achieved shape, and the humility of moon-watching was in her. But she'd received a shock, for instead of the white and perfected circle of the full moon she saw, low in the sky, a planet she could not recognize. She was afraid. What has gone wrong? she thought, and could not at first understand the lopsided crescent slung across the sky.

She called to Theron as he was coming upstairs, soon realizing that she was watching a lunar eclipse. She looked up her astronomy book and found tonight there was a partial eclipse.

Beth and Theron put on coats, took the binoculars and went out in the garden to observe the eclipse.

She lifted the heavy glasses and focused the lenses. The shadow of earth had fallen on the moon. Only a thin crescent of moon was left free, the rest of the full moon was dimmed to grey by the penumbra. A greenish light hung all around the moon and a red tinge also appeared close to the rim. The slant of the eclipse filled Beth with joy. I go through my eclipses also, she thought, the red rim is mine also, and she relished her childlessness. I am the one inhabiting the foam of my womb!'

After a few moments, Theron said, 'I'm cold, I'm going in.' Beth stayed out a little longer, gazing at the earth-shadow that was edging further across the moon. Then she shivered. The acreage of stars was too much for her, she felt giddy, a bit drunk. She went upstairs to bed and slept soundly until dawn, when she rose and went about the rooms and the garden, watching with delight as the sunlight washed the greyness from the world.

As she picks flowers, the giant speaks to Beth.

'A woman is a time machine; even when she is turning her head from side to side disagreeing with everything and everyone, a rhythm is diffusing through her, like moonspray rising and falling. Through the moon-time of woman, world-time gushes and stains.'

'Is it so, that I am timed by moons?' said Beth, aloud.

'You are moon-time,' says the giant, 'so why do you wear that wristwatch?'

Beth smiles.

'I'll keep my watch for a while,' she said, 'because I feel, giant, that behind the moon is a whip cracking which I must obey.'

'The whip is yours,' confided the giant, 'you must wield it, not jump to it. It is your own possession.'

Beth is silent, looking towards Giant Hill. Though she cannot see the giant for hedges, hills and plantations, she smells his spoors.

'My own possession . . .' she muses.

'Yes!' The Giant laughed. 'You were always faithful to me, Beth. I shall not abandon you. When Vellet committed her adulteries before my eyes, her veils ensnaring a brief moon, when the woman Vellet and her consorts danced on my prick, when she shouted: *"earth, moon, sun, stars, you'll never destroy me!"* when she danced lewdly, showing me her conspicuous vulva with its shining mucus, then I knew Vellet would need help one day. You must help her, Beth.'

Beth frowns, almost petulantly.

'So you say. Have said for ages! But why?'

'You know why, Beth. To help her complete her death, and to free Theron.'

'Theron! Oh he'll never let Vellet go. That is what I am beginning to think.'

'You must help Vellet. Then your husband will be free. Don't you want to rescue him?'

Beth is silent, sullen. The garden ceases to be a place of refuge.

'All loves will ease and resolve themselves when Vellet is free of her half-death,' says the giant quietly. 'Your loves, too, Beth.'

White clouds appear in the sky, a wind from the Atlantic begins to strut through the leaves. Beth picks up the mood of the wind and strides up and down beside the orchard fence, with long steps.

'You must grip the thorny veils that bind Vellet, grip them and tear them off,' instructs the giant.

'Won't I hurt my hands?' she whispers, fearfully.

'Perhaps,' says the giant. 'Yes, perhaps you will hurt your hands. Perhaps the skin of your lips will peel like old paint from a door and perhaps the night will shudder in its cradle. But the time cannot be postponed very much longer. Remember, Beth, in the giant's mirror, all broken creatures can be healed.'

'Why can't you heal Vellet, then?'

'I am healing her now. It is you who look into my mirror, and reflect. Vellet is blind to my mirror. I send you as my reflection, to that ghost, Vellet.' The giant speaks gently, reprovingly to Beth, and she flinches.

She walks slowly from tree to tree. The sky is cloudier. The branches move and sway in the wind.

'Beth! Hi, Beth! Beth!'

This new voice startles Beth, she shies round nervously, then smiling, hurries towards her visitor.

'Tabitha! Hello . . .'

'I'll just scribble a note for Theron, in case he comes home early.'

The two women go into the house through the conservatory, laughing and talking, relaxed in one another's company. In the kitchen, Tabitha perches on the table while Beth looks for paper and pencil. Beth is excited and thinks, soon it will be the longest day of the year.

She scribbles on the back of an envelope, 'gone for lunch to Tabitha's, back about four, love Beth.' She props the message up against the clock on the dresser, he is bound to glance at the clock; then she combs her hair, and is ready.

As the two women stroll along the lane, commenting on the clear sky, Tabitha remembers what her late husband once said to her. 'If I had as many women as I have valves in my heart, Tabitha, then I'd be happy, Tab, happy . . .' And then she'd felt his hands on her shoulders, heavy, dragging at her. Around her, the ruins of the abbey are still the man's allies. Now the sun is hot on her uncovered head.

Beyond the next turn of the path, the stream is glittery as forceps with the sun on the water. As they approach, Beth suggests that they sit down for a while. She pulls off her sandals and plunges her feet in the cold earthy water. She wriggles her toes in the water.

'It's lovely, Tabitha, lovely and cool.' Tabitha smiles and nods her head, but does not copy Beth.

'How have you been, Beth?' she asks, more seriously.

'Better for this sunny day,' Beth answers sleepily, stretching out full length on the grassy bank of the stream.

Tabitha sits upright and stares at the water. Last night her own screams, almost pure white with terror, had ransacked the house and even the hen-houses out in the backyard. What had she seen? Harry's eyes, like two silver thimbles stolen from the headmistress. Dead cats and dead children in his arms. Smiling, without feeling, as always. Up the big mountain of night, I went climbing with Harry. After I woke screaming, I didn't dare sleep again for fear my fingers would turn to mould. And I thought I was free of all that!

She looks down at her hands, frowning. Perhaps we have to give the dead some undamaged region in our hearts, and if this is not given, then the dead begin their impeachment. I am no longer so confident of my ability to walk backwards into the future and salvage what I need from it.

'What are you thinking about, Tab?' asks Beth drowsily.

'Ghosts, dear.'

Beth turns on her side and looks at Tabitha. Her wrists throb with questions. The questions rise up in her, she clutches at them before they become indecipherable.

'Why ghosts, Tab? That's unlike you.'

Tabitha hesitated, then said rapidly,

'The past two nights I've had bad dreams, nightmares. And this morning, early, with its beautiful gold light that seemed so fortunate, this morning, I opened the back-door and stepped out into the garden. And in the garden I saw hens and pheasants and colts and quails and rabbits and hares and turtles and elks and deer and asses and hounds and wolves and mallards and mares and oxen and goldfinches and tame swine and sheep and lions and herons and kine and foxes and geese and bears and goats and nightingales and horses and doves and kittens and moles and whelps and porpoises and ferrets and rooks and boars and apes and starlings and whales and larks and at the centre of this crazy menagerie, a man, amid the stench and cries.'

Beth moves closer to Tabitha.

'Who was the man?' she whispered.

Tabitha looks away and says, 'It was Harry. I saw his face. It was him. He smiled, raised his hand in greeting, waved, vanished, and all the animals too.'

Beth puts an arm around Tabitha's shoulders but Tabitha disengages herself gently and says, 'So it seems there are other ghosts beside little Vellet. What do you think?'

Beth shook her head slowly and the sunlight streamed off her body, as if repelled by a grease.

'I don't know, Tabitha. Perhaps it is all our own creation. That there are no ghosts, only us: the palpitations of our plagues, our own dark cupboards which aren't full of ghosts but only old clothes.'

'I think all husbands are called Lazarus,' says Tabitha roughly.

Beth smiles, then says firmly,

'We must not be trapped, we must read the runes of these apparent ghosts. What are they trying to tell us?'

Raising her eyes from Tabitha's frowning face, Beth saw on the opposite bank of the stream, Vellet, riding on her black hoyden horse with the docked tail, riding between the green branches, like doggerel. Beth's soothing advice dries on her tongue. But she does not point across the stream, does not ask Tabitha if she saw Vellet. Tabitha did not see Vellet, Beth is certain of that.

'I don't care what a ghost has to tell me,' protests Tabitha, 'why should I?'

Beth sighs and lies back on the grass again, looking up at the sky. That was what I said to the giant, she thinks. Why should I listen to the ghost, try to help the ghost. What are you called, Giant? she ponders. Giant Wheatland? Giant Cattle-Dung? Giant of the Ruins? Giant Cockcrow? Giant Blackmailer?

Beth looks up at the cloudless sky and thinks of clouds. Cumulus congestus, cumulus fractus, cumulus humilis and cumulus mediocris. The Giant may have his head in all of those clouds.

In the garden this morning Harry smiled at Tabitha from the richness of his animals and now Tabitha blushes, looks up at the clear sky and sees two martian moons. She smiles secretively, anarchic. Zatertag, a man's voice murmurs in her ear, Harry's voice.

In their separate cages of haunting, on a sunny morning, two bruised women sit by the water, watching butterflies; heartbeats of a marsh fritillary.

'I saw Harry,' says Tabitha in a low voice, 'and all his menagerie, and I took one step towards him and then all had gone, all but for my own chickens left scratching in the dust.'

Beth says, 'our wraiths are washed ashore.'

'Yes,' agrees Tabitha.

'What's happening, Giant?' yells Vellet furiously, 'what's happening?' She stamps her foot on the Giant's breast. 'What's Beth up to? Things are happening that I don't understand? Why isn't she afraid of me?'

The Giant said, 'look, Vellet.' She looks at the giant's open book and watches the pictures as he turns the pages for her.

'There's Theron!' she cried.

Theron is walking about the forbidden room, Vellet's room at the top of the house, the room that is dusty and unused. He is experiencing a nostalgia he cannot explain. He does not understand the emotion. But it could be the beginning for him of a life without Vellet. He glimpses a way out, and smiles.

Vellet gasps. 'Are they over?' she asks, 'are they over, Giant, the stiff miles of haunting? Is that what is happening to Beth, to all of us? Am I changing? Are we coming to a freer place?'

'I do not know,' said the Giant. 'I only reflect what you ghosts and lovers experience. Look at the pages of my mirror, Vellet.'

Now Theron is seated in an old leather armchair by the fireside in the forbidden room. He researches the past and the fogs that usually brood in his head clear. He thinks, perhaps I can make up my mind, decide which wife I want.

'Which wife does he want?' whispers Vellet.

'Hush,' says the Giant.

Theron opens the wardrobe door and takes out a long roll of paper. It is a poster. Carefully he unrolls the tube of paper and places a book at either end of the poster, laid flat on the table, so that it will not curl up again. He pores over the poster. It is a photograph of a drowned girl. It is a large coloured grainy photograph and the girl is very beautiful, cast up on the night shore, her short white dress plastered against breasts and thighs, her arms pinioned behind her. She is a woman undistinguished by fortitude or noble deeds. A woman drowned, unrescued.

'Ah,' groaned Vellet, 'he drowned me just as surely as if he'd pushed me in and held my head beneath the water.'

'Perhaps,' said the Giant calmly.

'Yes, he did,' said Vellet, 'look at the river-scars on my face, giant. He drowned me.'

'I know,' said the Giant.

Beneath Vellet's skin, stars leak.

'It will not be long, now, Vellet,' promised the Giant. 'They will let you go.'

The ghost wept. She wept, and hid beneath the floor of the summer house. She dug her cold fingernails into her heart and wept.

The Giant sends Vellet back to the living women, to study them, to learn from them.

Yes, thought Tabitha, with the sunlight drenching her skin and trickling through her bones. Yes, when Beth brought me her ghost story, I thought she was just compensating for a failed marriage, covering up the mess with a romantic story, the useful smokescreen of Vellet as ghost and revenger. But now my own strength is under attack, and my commonsense can't cope. The tide of my ghost is rising. I thought the dead faded away, with an expression of anger or of gratitude, into the pale green clay and our recollections. I told myself I had understood Harry's death, and adjusted. But I was wrong. In the darkest corner of the barn, he waits for me to let him go. To tell him it is time for him to depart. One word is required. But how can I say that word? What will I have left, if I cut the cord and let my ghost go? My muscles are stiff, my head is full of the sparse thoughts that follow an evening's drinking, and I see him still waiting in the musty shed, by the feed-bins, pouring grain through his hands, from one hand to the other, and back again. He has been there all the time but I have only been able to see him since Beth told me of Theron's relapsing ghost. Do I hate her for that? The unveiling she brought me? On the thin rim of my life, there is an arctic region where hate might exist, but I will not encourage it. What Beth has helped me to see, must be seen. I made a museum for Harry but he does not need it. I must travel up and down my own spine and unlock Harry from his bondage. I will let him go.

'I'll let him go,' she said aloud.

Beth looks at her sadly.

'It will not be easy,' she answers. 'For he'll require something of you before he is able to go. They see through all lies. It is only the true desire to free them that they can accept. Between their fingers and thumb they hold a key. Into us, they insert their key: and can only turn to freedom when the combination is correctly given. It is a process of learning for both ghost and haunted.'

Tabitha closes her eyes. 'I am very tired,' she says.

'Naturally, we are tired out by these guests,' says Beth gravely, 'but we invited them. We must endure them.'

Tabitha smiles.

'Do you think we can?' she asks eagerly.

'Yes,' says Beth firmly, 'I do.' And although Beth heard a sharp abrupt scream of anger, although she saw Vellet standing behind Tabitha, Vellet trembling in her wet and thorny veils, even though the ghost harangued Beth and spat at her, she did not flinch, she did not cry out to Tabitha, 'look out, behind you!', no, she adjusted her idea of the landscape so that she could accept the ghost, and with another howl, Vellet, confused and disappointed, merged into the hot summer air.

Beth and Tabitha go on their way, the ovary shadows of the women soft on the water. Beth crosses the stream, balancing barefoot on the stepping-stones.

'Be careful, it's slippery,' she warns Tabitha. When Tabitha has crossed over and stands close to Beth, smiling, Beth touches her shoulder timidly.

'Tabitha?' she says shyly.

'Yes?' The strain has eased from Tabitha's face, she is lighthearted again. 'Yes, dear?' she encourages Beth, 'what is it?'

Beth hangs her head and her hands are not real hands nor is her womb a real womb. But she must ask.

'Tabitha, I know this is asking a lot, and you've had a bad time lately, but please, do you think, can I, can I see Harry's paintings, please, please, it would be such a help to me, now . . .'

The words come out in a rush. Beth watches Tabitha anxiously. Sunlight drops slowly through Tabitha's head. She saw a shadow space-walking. A shadow. A shadow sucking the flowers. Tabitha recalls her aborted child wrapped in the robes of his blood. I must give, she cried inwardly, I must give Beth what she needs, must answer her hard request. This is a way of beginning to release Harry, the pain I experience is my own business, none of her concern. Yes, I will try to help Beth, so that she may cure the paraplegia that threatens her marriage. I will take my friend to my house and lead her upstairs, I will unlock that room for her, the room of deceptive calm. She agrees to Beth's request, agreeing to her own dethronement.

Beth sits at the old piano in Tabitha's parlour, playing and singing a Russian song. Tabitha stands by the window, thinking, over and over again, perhaps it was a shadow. Perhaps it was not Harry I saw but a shadow. It was a shadow. When Beth's song is finished, Tabitha turns and says, as if cursing Beth,

'Shall we go up, then?'

Tabitha unlocks the room where the paintings are hung, her mouth twisting, her wrists aching.

The two women enter a room as sad as the nursery built for Queen Catherine Parr's child.

A hot dry wind moves the stiff curtains. Tabitha stands by the door while Beth looks at each picture in turn. Tabitha watches her.

Hundreds of miles away, Ash is writing a letter to a blind lady.

Beth looks at the first painting: the intoxicated woman clutching her useless womb.

Tabitha watches intently, a woman who says 'no' in the language of the Saxons. Now she moves to the window, a polished stone, picked up from the shelf, in her left hand. She is smiling to herself, roughly playful with her own thoughts. On the brink of prison. Her back is turned to Beth now, straight, tense.

Beth is staring into the face of the drunken woman. Is this the one who will tell me what to do? I feel so strongly that in one of these paintings of Harry's, I'll find a message, an answer, the clue I need. The face of the drunken woman is only a waxwork, this is no answer. It is Tabitha as a younger woman. Horrible. The vomit on her lips, the womb where she burnt her fingers. Behind the drunk woman, a man walks to the block with the ambitious Lord Seymour. Beth peers into the shadows of the painting. Vellet, by her side, holds her breath. Beth glances at Vellet and smiles. Vellet, unsmiling, whispers to Beth, 'not this one, no, not this one.' Beth shrugs. 'I know. But which one then?' Vellet vanishes. Beth turns away from the twilight of the drunken woman.

Tabitha has descended to the second degree of her soul. She is the waxwork widow. She hears Beth's footsteps on the wood floor as she moves to the next painting.

The griffons with necks like snakes squat on the book of love.

Tabitha thought, he abused my undergarments. Then I heard a death cry from the garden. I heard the shot. I found him with his head blown in. There was blood on the shells of the snails that crawled over the rose trees.

Beth craned her neck, trying to read the words on the page of the book of love, and gets a shock. '. . . *he whipped her with his sodomite's whip.*'

Beth half turns and says, 'Tabitha?'

But Tabitha does not turn from the window, does not answer,

and Beth dare not ask her a question. The griffons glare but Vellet says, 'not these creatures, Beth.'

He wrote a scholarly monograph on medieval pigments, thought Tabitha with the old amazement, but he shot himself through the head just the same.

Beth moves on and looks at the female saint sipping menstrual blood in a shadowed place. A homespun woman with a monthly thirst. Beth smiles at the saint. This saint, she thinks, could open the door to the waterfall and proceed through the wondrous waters. Is this the answer? Is this the way to find an honest answer for Vellet? To help Theron? To enable me to understand Ash?

Beth would like this to be the painting. In the shadows are alpine flowers and huge boulders. Tabitha lights a cigarette, inhales, rattles the box of matches in her hand. The polished green stone gleams on the windowsill. She puts the matches down, picks up the stone again, still warm from her hand.

Beth smiles at the saint. To her eyes, the saint's face is that of Ash on the verge of orgasm, the deadline of delight. *And there I saw four and twenty damsels*, thinks Beth joyfully, *embroidering satin at a window.*

I slipped my hand into the hollow tree trunk, recalls Tabitha to herself, I unfolded the scrap of paper on which he'd scrawled, meet me in Black Hill Barn tonight. I tore the message up but kept the appointment. I kissed the bark of the hollow tree. I arrived on schedule. Not even the evidence of shadows made me unhappy in those days. In my mind's eye, I still see my hand, blue-white as a blown egg, hovering over the latch of the barn door. I entered the barn and instead of him, it was Harry waiting for me, his one-eyed vigilance that broke my bones.

Beth and the saint still commune. There is a fountain in this shadowy garden of the saint. The waters spring, noble blood. Beth imagines herself kneeling naked beside the bloody fountain, and that a bull of gold and a unicorn of ice appear beside her. Dark toads with lamenting cries approach. The saint strokes my shoulders, irresolute but able.

'No, Beth, no. It is not here, what you are looking for.'

Vellet warns Beth to move on, showing her white teeth. Vellet is a wanderer from the prison-places, Vellet of the Seven Scars. She must be listened to . . .

Tabitha stubbed out her cigarette. She stared out of the window but did not see the giant. She did not see the daughters of the giant, alphabetical in their robes. She did not see the sun shining on the fields. She does not consider gathering bluebells in the moonlit valleys. She imagines strangers laughing at the crude jokes they have made about her. The room has thrown its noose around her throat and it is tightening. Harry said to her, I'll plant babies in the cabbage patch for you, Tab!

Beth glances casually at the study of lovers, Harry and Tabitha. On my way here, she thought, I knew this was not the painting. The orchard is too perfect, the lovers too accomplished. Lovers at dawn, seeking the wild ox's alchemy, do not help Beth. But she enjoys the painting even though it is not her solution. As she turns away, the lovers' laughterless shadows tell her, you are one of the descendants of the children of Hamelin.

Very likely, thought Beth, amused.

'Move on, move on,' urged Vellet.

Tabitha is afraid of this room. Her whole body itches and sweats. Harry said to her, there are fifty empty milk bottles under the sink but I cannot move them, because that would mean I am manipulating reality, and I cannot do that.

'Move on, Beth.'

Beth confronts the final painting. It is the largest canvas. It is of Jesus and the Virgin.

Tabitha lays one hand on each breast. There is a pain like infanticide in her body. Frost blackens her summer garden. I am hammering my omens into shape. Behind my back, Beth is learning what she came to find out. The tribes of the sea flow through me and I am lonely as a bow and arrow. Water laps against my closed doors.

In the painting the Virgin holds a fish in her hand. The Virgin is veiled. Beth stands very still. She does not panic. But she is crawling towards knowledge, not walking upright.

The torches of Tabitha's mind are flickering, a black basket of candles. Autumn will not help her. Blindfolded wives wave at her in the halfblood storm. My dark takes many shapes. Rectum or vagina he said I don't care I said he wound a cloth tightly round my mouth so I could not shout blasphemous words Harry gave me two coins he shaved my cunt with his razor he refused to believe in anything supernatural he painted his face with rouge a chill settled on the wife for her lifetime beheaded cold jointure the ghost gave off sparks when struck I waited for him he was late he had been working he said I withdrew my complaint . . .

'I see,' cried Beth suddenly, excitedly, 'I see!'

'Yes,' said Vellet softly, 'you see, now you see.'

Beth runs across to Tabitha and pulls her towards the painting of Jesus and the Virgin. Tabitha allows herself to be dragged in front of the canvas.

'Look,' said Beth, 'it's incredible, it is what we were saying this morning, how the ghosts grow together. Look, do you see, haven't you ever noticed?'

Beth points at the Virgin, she is trembling with her discovery.

'What is it?' asks Tabitha, exhausted, afraid.

'Haven't you ever noticed? Look at the Virgin's face. Beneath the veil. Don't you recognize her?'

Tabitha goes up close to the painting and studies it closely.

'I still don't see what you mean, Beth.'

Beth fidgets about the room, amazed at Tabitha's blindness. Vellet watches the two women wistfully.

'Look,' urged Beth, 'look!'

Tabitha looked. She saw.

She groaned. 'Oh god!' she groaned. In that early spring Harry had knocked at her skull and then gone out to his studio to paint this . . . Tabitha hears again the crude laughter she hated years ago and the polished green stone turns cold again in her hand.

Vellet watches her compassionately, watching as Tabitha pulls the painting off the wall and throws herself to the floor with it, tearing at the canvas with her fingernails. Vellet watches as Beth struggles to pull Tabitha to her feet, to save the painting from her destructive hysteria, watches Beth slap Tabitha and try to hold her down. She listens to Tabitha's screamed obscenities and observes Tabitha fight Beth off. Beth, unable to stop Tabitha from weeping and yelling, runs in a panic downstairs and out of the cottage, the door catching to behind her. Tabitha stretches full length on the floor, writhing and banging her head repeatedly, then staggering to her feet and tearing her clothes off, stripping to her skin and rolling on the floor again. Vellet watches her own face, disguised as the Virgin. Tabitha spits on that face over and over again. Vellet, the Virgin. Vellet, the artist's model and mistress. She watches the canvas curl up in the shadows where Tabitha has hurled it. She watches Tabitha limp out of the room and into her bedroom, where she takes two pills and crawls into bed.

Beth meanwhile is running home thinking: connected with death connected with death we must be connected with death Tabitha must understand that she cannot ignore it she must let the nocturnal visitors in I tell her she must love the dead her hair dark as a parsee her mouth wide and shrieking her face dark and thin I was so frightened her splotchy skirt her hands grown cold from weaving ropes for the hanged I could do nothing to help her connected with death we must be connected with death her hysteria is below the threshold of my heart her hatred invaded my moon she must let the dead in and accept them I was right to show her that Vellet was the Virgin she must have known all the time but never let herself look at it but only let the whisper perch by her heart she will understand when she recovers she must not let herself be defeated how she screamed but it is not a battle all this trouble it is a learning my children will need my children need it to become alive and bright with flower and flute . . . if I can live with my dead and study their shadows in clean rooms if I can give the eyelids their chance to live in pentagrams of blood . . .

So Beth thinks, as she runs home through the sunlit woods, Vellet loping by her side, keeping pace.

TWENTY TWO

VELLET the Virgin.
Vellet, the Virgin!
Beth tramps through the sunlit trees, rejoicing, amazed, a bezonian woman watching great changes in herself, in all around her. I have found the key! I have discovered the clue.
'Perhaps,' murmurs Vellet demurely.
'It is the harvest of Orion!' cries Beth, and her shadow falls lightly on the genitals of the spider.
'Perhaps,' Vellet coos.
I saw the Virgin's face beneath the veil of grey-blue paint and her features were those of Vellet. Vellet, the ghost with her epidemic of love-bites, Vellet, the faithless wife with her drugs and her albino bowels, Vellet always tracing out the skidmarks of her marriage. How I have hated her, hated her soothsayer's feet dancing over our bodies, hated her keys of belladonna opening our eyes when we should have slept, Theron and I. Always, her tantalus presence in our garden. I have hated her. I have been the dorsal bride to her ventral, I have trembled with rage in Theron's arms, dancing with him only a pessimist's waltz. From the moment she emerged in the dark rainy lane, I have hated Vellet.
Theron hates her. He hates her shadowy riots. He puts his head out of the window, say, and she is always there on the lawn, grinning up at him. Vellet Frithborn, her hectic skeleton gleaming in the wolf-pack's dark. She has shown him her brochure of tall stories, made him follow her calendar. And he hates her.
Beth slows down and dawdles across a field of dandelions.
We have hated Vellet, she thinks, but have we the right?
'I was not allowed to choose my death,' says Vellet. But Beth does not hear her. She is deafened by the shock she received in Tabitha's house, amid the paintings, and now the aftermath of Tabitha's hysteria is making her feel queer and lightheaded. What I have

discovered may still be an undeliverable letter. I have yet to explain to Theron the significance of Vellet as Virgin: to convince him of the sadness of the ghost: to teach him we must love Vellet before she can be free and we free of her. We are both too used to hating Vellet to find that love will come easily. We have our implacable side, each of us. We may be at a standstill between love and hate for some time yet; yet I have seen her true face now, her other face. And I know that soon I will be able to love her. A virgin, a little goddess, a transformed one.

Beth stands rapt by the field gate. The hot sun bathes her. The trees are without wild ancestors. The blue sky is all tender execution.

Vellet stands sadly beside Beth. Beth cannot see her yet. The translucent ghost is becoming shabby. She watches Beth and is apprehensive. Vellet is grasping the fact of her disfigurement, is beginning to long for and yet also to fear the next stage of her death, that substance of emotions with which Beth and Theron will disinfect her and send her on her journey. Vellet is frightened, thinking, they will tear me limb from ghost-limb, there is no other possibility, my dislodgement will hurt more than my death.

Beth climbs over the gate and continues home across the flaming landscape. I can teach Theron to love her! she thinks excitedly, to love her!

Vellet trails disconsolately behind Beth. Words in her mouth are something she has forgotten.

And still, amid the fieriness of the afternoon, there remains icy material in Beth's head that will not thaw. All at once a sickness heaves into her stomach, turning her hopes and ambitions into a grainy semaphore. Poor Tabitha! she thinks, and approaches the stream gloomily, sitting at the water's edge. Poor Tabitha. I have taken too much from her. I have taken her carefully constructed survival from her, left her desolate among the unclean animals of the bible. I have shown her Harry's last insult, his fifteen year old mistress painted in the guise of the Virgin. I have let uninvited guests into Tabitha's head, let the ghost get to her. How many years has she been fending off that ghost? Must she now return to that twilight where Harry waits for her, laughing. Should I have spared her that, let her go on with her unblemished life, fearing nothing. I don't know. It seemed there was no choice. When I realized that the Virgin was Vellet, the shock and joy of my discovery went through me like a leap in which I turned head over heels and alighted firmly on my feet, I thought that Tabitha too would benefit from this knowledge, find it a doorway into a region of steady light and clearer understanding. For her it came too late? Perhaps.

'Vellet, how could you pose for Harry as the Virgin?' asks Beth, half-amused, half-reproving the ghost who is tapdancing on the waters that are like a sheet of glass in the sunlight.

'I can draw a full-size goose egg through any lady's wedding ring,' remarks Vellet, and slips invisible into a notch of sunlight.

Beth sits alone by the waters, quietly thinking of Ash. Of Ash at the green throat of this same stream. Of the slight pause between the two sentences Ash used to say goodbye. Felling Beth with her unknown language.

TWENTY THREE

He gazes into the folds of fire. The dry garden refuse makes a good bonfire safely contained in the square mesh box of the incinerator. He watches, relaxed, enjoying the odour of garden-smoke, with its atmosphere of mild untruths.

It is cool now in the evening. Theron is glad of the cooler air that hovers behind the heat of the bonfire. The morning and afternoon had blazed like that bonfire and he and Beth sheltered indoors all day, out of the strong heat. It was at the tips of their fingers like explosions. But indoors they were calm and resourceful. Beth prepared a cold lunch, a salad. She has a natural aptitude for this. The wine was white and very cold. Beth's serenity transmitted itself to him and in her shelter of cool calmness he felt safe. He smiles, and stares at his hands caked with earth. He looks about his garden with pleasure, the smooth lawns, the well-kept flowerbeds, the roses, the staunch hedges clipped and shaped into animal-forms. He is at peace with himself and his world.

The fire crackles and grumbles, a chattering of incognitos. Within the flames is the possibility of munitions, he thought suddenly, and he saw flame-throwers directed on the bodies of soldiers. The folds of fire contain all the colours of last month. The grey smoke has a sheen like a valuable fur and as Theron stares he sees that Vellet is the grey creature of smoke rising slowly from the flames.

'No,' he says. 'No, not today, Vellet, don't spoil it.' He backs away from her.

She goes on rising from the flames. He turns, runs to get the hose, douses the fire, but she is still in the garden, over there, by the fuchsias.

'What of my unborn son, Theron?' she appeals to him.

'I don't know,' he stammers, the smoke arid in his throat.

Vellet delves into her long smouldering hair and laughs.

'Death is but the midpoint of a long life,' she quotes.

'Don't come near me,' he said menacingly. But he knew it would make no difference. She would come towards him, with her hottentot shadow, her gravest smoke. She will write 'hallucinosis' on his tongue. 'Sleepy sickness', she whispers in his ear. Between the dying fire and the coming shadows, he can hardly breathe. 'I hate you,' he told the ghost. 'I know,' she said, 'that is the trouble,' and her eyelids were immobile, her tongue divided snakily at its end.

Indoors, Beth is closing the windows against the chill of twilight. Then she turns on the table lamp and begins her small imperfect stitches.

Theron's hands are dirty but Vellet's are clean, her fingers white, scrubbed. 'Get away from me,' he moaned. Vellet takes his hand. She leads him into the summer house. He is afraid and his mind is full of the echoes of pain, of the frozen, of the burnt. Vellet smells of imprisonment and when she comes close to him he does not see her face but the hideous mask of an old woman. She presses up against him and he closes his eyes. His little finger aches with cold but his cock throbs with heat. He began to recite the names of stars aloud, to keep him from capitulating, 'Mesarthim, Algenib, Tarased, Adhara, Mirsam, Jabbah, Mintaka,' but as he stammers the list, he hears Vellet laughing, and her body is pressed against him, her damp shawl oozing over him, and he pulls up her grey-green dress to rub himself against her misty thighs. Carefully he buries himself in the reeds of her cunt and begins to fuck the ghost.

Beth hears Vellet wailing from beneath the waters. She runs out into the garden. Where is Theron? She pauses by the blackened cinders of the bonfire and listens. She hears sounds from the summerhouse and is already weeping herself. The beard growing beneath her legs bristles. She goes helplessly and angrily to the threshold.

Her husband is wanking inside the summerhouse. Beth watches him. Theron takes no notice of her. Some people seem to be whispering behind Beth's back. She watches, as if seeing all this in a mirror. As she watches Vellet gradually seeps into view. Beth sees how Vellet has fitted her ghost vagina over Theron's prick.

'Theron, you are being tricked,' said Beth sadly. Vellet looks at Beth scornfully, her black wings held stiff and high, and then becomes invisible again so Beth can only see Theron jerking himself off. He licks his lips and groans, 'Vellet, Vellet,' and comes, his spunk flicks out across the summerhouse wall. He sighs, wipes his fingers on his pants.

'This won't do,' said Beth, deeply concerned for him.

'Shit on you!' said her husband, turning away, zipping his fly.

'Look,' she said, 'can't we talk? Vellet isn't real and . . .'

He pushed her to one side and left her alone in the little stuffy shed.

Vellet watches the metal bird moving in the night wind, first north, then east, south, west. She watches Beth weep. She wants to say something to Beth but she is afraid of her and creeps out into the fields. She rests in the giant's hand, her eyes wide open.

Beth stops weeping and says to herself, he thinks he can do anything, does he, just because he has married me with wine and water, cunt and prick, but I am not staying with him much longer! Let him complete his own jigsaw puzzle! Her anger makes her a bit tipsy, she digs her fingernails into her forearms, her thin skirt feels icy against her legs. I may have to abandon this whole business as too difficult, she thinks, smiling tensely at her earlier optimism. She is in shock though. She cannot forget the white sperm pumping out thick and warm. She feels that her mouth is enormous, that she has swallowed some peculiar large object, perhaps something alive. Her repressed excitement at the memory of Theron's orgasm grows like a pale light in the darkness. All this goes beyond the demands of a dowry, she thinks. When she passes Theron's window, she can see him standing naked, looking out at her. Her skeleton moving like dew, she comes indoors, upstairs, towards him, and, her mind stopping and starting, she pulls him against her hip, begins panting, half-weeping. They make love standing up, without words. Her orgasm is chill and foggy. Afterwards, Beth is afraid of the dark thoughts of the giant. She looks at Theron, sprawled asleep on the bed, then turns away, goes to the bathroom to sponge her cunt with warm water.

TWENTY FOUR

IN the church there is a cruel gold eagle who carries a book shouldered upon its wings. There is a green satin cloth of embroideries bursting into flower and star. Stained-glass men and women are looking at a woman sitting in a pew, she is like a piece of broken colourless glass, alone in the church.

The sunset presses her into folds of stone. She has come here to learn which part of her life to choose: the past or the future. But there is no answer here, just as there was no answer in the familiar room where a dim light burnt, no answer in the summer darkness, nor the close-calls of sleep.

Late this afternoon, she sat in a wicker garden chair beneath a tree whose long slender pliant branches dipped into the water of the pond, and watched the wild waterfowl pluck the surface, drawing folds of shadowy water in their wake, unconcerned, at ease. The sky grew cloudy and rain threatened, she heard the wind in the branches, like the faint singing of old men.

The chair creaks, it is old, discoloured by sunlight and rain.

The wind moves slowly and gradually across the pond, the reeds, the branches of the willow and the bones of the seated woman. She reproaches herself for her inaccurate thin garments and rising from her chair, she walks back to the house, with no answer.

The book she was reading lies forgotten on her chair. The wind flicks the pages over, the words are broken up. Now night will read this book.

Ash went out into the rainy sunset and sat in the church.

When she left, the rain had stopped. She walked aimlessly and came eventually to a tawdry new block of flats. In the courtyard that opened out on to the highway stood a group of nude cupid-like children who looked at her silently.

She walked on, aware of a decision at the edge of her mind. She remembered the story Jake once told her, after they'd quarrelled, and after she'd listened, the bitterness of moons became apparent to her.

She paused, glanced back to see the group of children, but the road was empty, no figure, trees or animals.

She came to a decision then, walked on rapidly for several moments, stopped, heaved open the door of the phone box, fumbled in her pocket for a coin and for Beth's number, and dialled.

Darkness gathers up hot pence, the stars.

Ash sits by the open window and waits. She is no longer afraid of the consequences of flight. She waited until Jake had gone to work and then she had driven the children to the house of a friend, Ruth, whose children were roughly of an age with Ash's. She told Ruth, I have to go away, it's an emergency, can you . . . ? Ruth nodded, then leaned forward and kissed her.

She drove away, knowing Jake would pick the kids up that evening or the next day. But without hesitating, she drove to the station, and now waits in Beth's old house, for a message, for an arrival. She feels tipsy, her nightdress sticks to her sweaty body.

If she does not come, thinks Ash, or if she rejects me, then I must go back to Jake. But I had to take the chance. I felt the time had come to return here. I need to know what drew us together five summers ago, whether it is still vital to us, or whether it is only our memories we need to refresh, not our lives. We both have to be free, surely, to get this business clear.

I come here as a messenger, and I may be bringing snow into her summer.

When I got out of the taxi and looked up at the house, I was depressed by the neglected garden, the grimy windows. But then I accepted my responsibility for the dilapidation of our landscape. I should have visited sooner. I should have written, answered Beth's letters.

But I could not. I had turned away. The journey of the gamete bubbled its heat through me and would not let me write letters, or think of myself in any other role but that of mother, wife.

Now the melting flesh of my month browses deep in me, as I

wait. My belly aches. I recall Beth and myself, our smiles impaled upon old photographs.

In this house, my white downy thoughts go about their duties, just as I went about the house, removing the dust sheets, opening the windows, letting the fresh air and the sun in, cleaning the grimy mirrors, restocking the larder. The electricity was off, but the warm air is drying the house out, and I've lit the kitchen range so that the night does not chill and spoil my work.

I'd gone straight to the old outhouse when I arrived, and there, as always, the spare key hung on its hook in the darkest corner. I let myself into the house and touched surfaces, mantlepiece, stopped clock, poker, cupboard door. I left my fingerprints everywhere.

Veiled faces of myself watched me from the past as I cleaned and scrubbed the years away. In the thicket of a bedroom I saw myself with a bunch of thin flowers from the moorland clutched in my hand. My younger selves dappled the mirror's vault. Never once have I seen Beth's new image in the house I am reclaiming for us. She must bring that reflection with her. It is that I am waiting for. I am at a crossroads. Only contact with this house, with Beth, will show me which of the offered roads I am to take.

A wingless rain is falling now, the heat of storm recedes. The rain is very slight, inexperienced. It reminds me of my children's tadpoles, earlier this year. The tadpoles jerked, carnivorous, in their moonstruck waters. I remember them, their pensive heads and witty tails. I have been moving myself about slowly, piece by piece in these rooms. It is as if I have been eaten into by moths and my skin frays in my hands. The house is clean and alive once again and yet I can smell decay in myself, the canals and cavities of my body. Their mucous nature puzzles me.

I do not know which way to turn now, not to the rain, nor to the reflections. The rain smells of minnows and leaves. I want to belong to myself. Will Beth show me how?

The desperately unhappy events of last weekend, the fighting with Jake, turned my life into an area of land sown with mines. I could not remain among those mishaps until I came back to the place where I was most myself.

On the phone Beth was guarded. She would hardly say anything. I do not know what welcome she will give me.

I estimate the smallest possible amount of sadness I can expect to experience from my return, and I find it is too large for me.
I could leave tomorrow.
But will not.
I will sleep. Perhaps I will dream of a world without flying creatures, no eagles, doves, sparrows or humming birds. There the men and women are clear-sighted, unenchanted by the furling of feathers, never saddened like me by the aerodynamics of birds soaring above ruins into the blue, the open sky.

Next morning, long before Ash wakes in the old house, Beth drives slowly through the empty village streets, past the church, past the pubs, past Tabitha's shuttered cottage. The car moves almost stealthily through the dawn.

That dead girl in the summerhouse. She is sharper than a sword and thinner than a hair, thinks Beth. I am much afraid of summer and Vellet. It is a combination that has proved too strong for me. I've thought and worried about Vellet so often and I thought I was just about to solve the problem she set us, but I was wrong about all that.

When I said to Theron, 'but I saw the painting, and Vellet was the Virgin, don't you see? There are other aspects of Vellet we've not even begun to consider yet, we've limited her by our own narrow perceptions, and we've driven her to act out a baneful ghost's drama because that is our drama, not hers. If we can allow ourselves to love Vellet, we'll all be free . . .' he turned away, shaking his head. 'I don't see what this has got to do with me,' he said, 'It is your illumination, Beth. It works for you, fine, ok. But I am still in the dark.'

Theron turned his back on me, on my attempt to explain the ghost to him. He went away to look for his own solution. Perhaps I was wrong. Perhaps Vellet posed as the Virgin with a cynical jokey attitude, and she has fooled me. But I cannot believe that. The purity and grace of her expression could not be a fraud. It was true, and shone out.

Beth drives like an automaton, her destination known and terrifying.

The phone had rung and it was Ash and I thought that death is like this. 'I want to see you, Beth.'

I could hardly stammer out an answer, just said she must go on up to the old house.

My heart, newly exposed to the air, turned brown. There is no certainty that a white raven won't be found tomorrow, though past experience would make such an occurrence unlikely.

Ash.

Her voice pierced me. I am afraid now.

The first crest of sunlight appears on the hills, at this time of acute danger. The yellow tint creeps forward, making narrow inlets on the grey. Gates, fences, tractors in fields, horses grazing, distant farmhouses on hilltops are sharpening in outline. Their shapes fill out, a jigsaw puzzle rising out of the grey dawn.

Suddenly she pulled the car off the road and parked on the hard shoulder close to a patch of common land. She opened the car door and stepped out into the odours of dawn. There is still mist in Yellcombe Mead and the thin trees of Morning Well Plantation are only just emerging. Daylight is a loud noise in Beth's head. Dawn had hidden her but now she is out in the open, exposed.

She begins to climb uphill over the rough grass.

Lifelong maps are written on her hands.

When she reaches the top of the ridge, she hears a woman crying for help. She looks all around the empty fields, up at the pale inbred sky, up at the moon. Who called out, 'Help me'? Who?

As Beth stands on the hilltop in the early dank sunlight, she hears the murmurings, mutterings, hummings and whisperings of many women all around her. The sound rises to a crescendo, a burliness that mocks Beth, and then suddenly cuts out, leaving only silence with no escape. Silence, like a hole scooped in the ground.

Beth is alone. Those women are elsewhere. And she could not make out the words they were uttering. Something about standing between the victim and the knife? Beth shrugs, angered. She stands on the edge of the hill and rolls her imaginary children down, like cheeses.

Which way now, Beth? She is gasping for breath. Which way?

Blue sky and mauve hills, brown fields, landscape like a manuscript containing a later writing written over an effaced earlier script. Which way?

Beth is sobbing and throws herself full-length on the damp grass. I am finished with impersonations. I can no longer be a wife mediating between ghost and husband. I must go back to my own perception of myself.

She scatters the words of her wedding on the ground and then she runs, fast as she can, across fields, ditches, over streams, running, for she must catch up with the shadow at the edge of the giant, or he'll tie her veins together.

She falls to the ground, tripping, she is within the boundary of the giant, out of breath she crawls forward and kisses his chalky penis.

'Help me, Giant, before I grow any weaker. The naked baby blocks my path, lisping, Beth, carry me, carry me. I do not want to. Help me, Giant. Look, I can pay, I have money. Look in my purse. I have denarii and sovereigns, guilders and half-marks, sesterces and one louis-d'or. I have dollars and kopecks, nickels and sequins, centaros and farthings. Look.'

'Put your money away, Beth, and look in my mirror, instead. Look.'

Beth looks where the giant points. When the reflections settle, she sees herself running along a dim gallery in an old house. No, it is not her. It is Vellet. Vellet turns and smiles. The mirror clouds, then clears to show a man gutting a fish. It is Theron. He does not speak and does not hear Beth call.

'I don't understand,' said Beth.

'Watch,' said the giant. 'One of my pictures will answer you. Wait. When it comes you will know it.'

In the mirror Beth sees the face of her grandchild.

She sees herself going on a pilgrimage, a steel collar around her neck.

Theron steps forward from the mirror and mouths inaudibly at her.

A lazy girl plays the guitar fretfully.

A morning of serpents, a room of women.

The reflections gather and break up, reform.

A small white room where Jesus and his mother wait.
Beth's mother, cracking open the sun.
Night: armies of the moon turning to cold water.
Beth flinging herself down on the bed and the man beside her speaking of ghosts.

In the giant's mirror two rooms are reflected: one room is untidy, daubed with clothes, books, records, unanswered letters. The second room is clean and neat. A girl stands in each room, each girl is nursing a newborn baby. Beth passes from one room to the other, singing a peace treaty. The girl in the untidy room is bitter. But the girl in the white clean room smiles and says, are you clothed in skin and flesh, now, Beth?

'I have not seen my solution yet,' said Beth to the giant.

'Then go on watching,' he said.

Beth's eyes are sore but she goes on watching.

She saw herself and Theron standing side by side in a ploughed field, a concourse of seabirds circling above their heads. It had been a time of happiness then, even though she knew he would break his promises.

Other pictures: angels dredging the sky, Tabitha wearing an old-fashioned dress the colour of oysters. A man setting fire to himself. Beth diving into the left ventricle of the apostle's heart. Rooms flashing past. Moons hoeing the sky. Fountains, where girls wait averting their faces, murmuring windswept words. A figure of a man made of compressed snow that stands all day on the lawn. A child's toy that rattles when shaken. And to each picture Beth says firmly, not this, not this, not this.

A group of six women are standing beneath the rose-window in the church.

'What is this?' says Beth.

The women are Eve, Sarah, Tamar, Rhahab, Ruth, Bathsheba.

Eve asks Sarah for a handkerchief.

Sarah plaits Tamar's hair.

Tamar laughs at Rhahab's joke.

Ruth looks serious.

Bathsheba dips her fingers in the font.

Bathsheba points to the man of letters, silent in his wooden cage, and cries,

What is his answer?

He has no answer. This makes the women restless. They want to leave the church. But the doors are locked.

Who locked the doors?

When Ruth dared to open the sealed order they read, lock the doors. Who locked the doors?

It is cold and damp in the church. Outside, autumn is calming down the trees.

Whose blood stains the altar cloth?

Bathsheba says, not mine.

Tamar says, not mine, not mine.

Ruth laughs and says, not mine, not mine, mimicking exasperation.

Sarah shouts, not mine.

Rhahab swigs from a can of beer, then says, not mine.

Eve is silent and her five companions watch her.

It is mine, she says, the blood is mine.

The six women swing round rapidly and stare out of the mirror towards Beth. They all wear the same face now. Beth recognizes the face. It is the face of Ash, repeated six times, weaving back into the mirror, until the mirror has gone, sunk back into the green turf, and Beth is alone with the Giant.

Without a word to him, she stumbles downhill. The giant looks about him in an abstracted listless manner, with the eyes of an old horse. Vellet, approaching from the direction of the river, does not dare speak to him, creeps back to the water.

TWENTY FIVE

THE giant has unlocked his mirror.

Beth will meet her reflection. She will cross to the other side of the mirror. She will enter the abyss of the mirror.

On other occasions rain and sperm have made Beth's fingers wet but now it is sweat that makes her hands slippery.

She gets out of the car, trembling. Why does the house look different? Why are the windows open? Why is the door open?

Beth knows the answer to her questions.

Who waits for me in my house?

She knows. Ash waits.

On the threshold, Beth prepares herself for the meeting. She is very frightened. What if it has all been an illusion, my recollection of a perfect season, of Ash's beauty? Suppose the girl I remember is changed and lost? What if the girl Ash remembers has gone away, in some dark nebula?

The sun has risen, it is long past dawn. This is terrible, thinks Beth, I don't want to meet her, it will hurt far too much, I am going to turn and run.

But she stumbles into the hallway. After the brightness of day, Beth is blind in the dark passageway. Through the darkness of the house, down the stairs, someone is coming.

'Who are you?' asks Beth sharply.

'Don't you recognize me?' said the other woman quietly, coming closer.

This woman is wearing gentle yet chaotic colours. In her hand she carries a half-eaten apple. Beth looks at her and as her eyes grow accustomed to the shadows, she sees in the stranger, no stranger. Beth looks at Ash for the first time and for the thousandth time. She shares the ceremony of courage Ash is inaugurating, by coming to this house. She sees Ash and all Ash implies. Yet she dare not move towards Ash, to elicit the first greeting.

Beth turns away, she has seen that Ash is flawless.

It is too much for Beth. She feels like an outcast. Twice she tries to speak to the woman who is watching her silently, compassionately. But twice she fails, twice savage waves of sweat debauch her and chill her to silence. She hears her silence like the clatter of an iron key on the stone floor of the kitchen. The stupidity of her silence echoes around them.

She opens a door and walks into a room without looking back at Ash. This room has always been called the library, although there are not nearly enough books here to warrant the title. Beth feels she will be safer in here, hidden from this strange summer. The room smells of polish, and fresh flowers. The dust has been swept away, the windows are cleaned. Beth peers at the books on the shelves, long-out-of-fashion novels, obscure biographies, foreign dictionaries, all taken asylum here.

Ash is standing in the doorway.

Beth takes a deep breath. She likes this room's quiet, she had forgotten this was her favourite room. She takes a book from the shelf, reads at random.

'What is that book?' asks Ash in a low voice.

'Descriptions of old gardens,' says Beth, tense again. She feels Ash's hand on her shoulder and turns to see in Ash's grey eyes the promise of an unskimped friendship. Beth trembles and she moves out of the shadow as she hears Ash say again,

'Don't you recognize me, Beth?'

Beth nods.

'Yes,' she whispers. 'I know you. But I am afraid now. You are too much of a phantom. I've thought about you so much that it doesn't seem possible to me that you too look back at our time together longingly. I am at a loss. Your phone call shocked me with its reality. You have been a dream to me. Perhaps you should go away before we are both hurt.' But Beth says this last half-heartedly.

Ash smiles.

'Go away? Of course not.'

'But I'm afraid, Ash.'

'I'm afraid too,' said Ash, 'what of it?' When Ash touches her, Beth feels that her own body has taken on the shape of a giantess.

Her thoughts are cold, a garden of needles. She hears the voices of defiled heroes telling myths and legends. Ash's fingers stroke Beth's hair, recalling Jake's eyes speckled with silver as if he had never seen Ash before, as if her sex were still to be named and learned. Ash sighs and urinates shadow. Beth is relaxing, leaning against Ash, her limbs no longer grotesque.

Hugging tightly, the women stumble upstairs. In the bedroom at the top of the stairs, Ash takes Beth's hand and kisses her forefinger. Beth and Ash stand naked in the shadow of the mirror. Their bodies move together in a cumulus. Embracing rediscovered flesh, they bite breasts, they kiss cunts. 'I am piecing you together,' gasps Ash. Beth catches her breath. The two women tremble on the edge of carnival then fall slowly into a silent bed, a grey raft in the room.

Afterwards, in the sunlit room, Ash sleeps soundly but Beth falls into a torpor and does not know what thoughts she is thinking or why.

When they wake, it is late morning and rain is streaming down the window-panes.

Rain streams across the mirror of the giant. The predictions of fine weather have not come true. But the women are immune to weather today. They are still piecing one another together, gathering up the lost fragments.

Splashing and singing, they bath together. The steam on the bathroom mirror hides nothing from them.

'I knew you'd come! I knew you'd come to me!' crows Ash happily.

Beth smiles and squeezes the sponge between her legs. She has no regrets. Her long hair is wet through, it is plastered against the nape of her neck and her shoulder-blades. She leans forward and looks into the far-reaching regions of Ash's eyes. Ash does not look away. She stares at Beth, concentrating in turn on her friend's features.

Outside, the summer trees carry the rain easily in their thick foliage. The white five-pointed flowers are whiter in the rain.

Beth says, 'the day after you and Jake left, years ago, I went into the village and the first person I met was an elderly lady who was selling small paper flags, to be worn as a sign of having given to charity. I bought one of those flags. I still have it, it is in my purse. I took the pin out and kept the flag.'

'All that time,' Ash murmurs, 'I was busy with other things...'

Beth trickled the warm soapy water through her fingers.

'Yes,' she said softly, 'yes. After you'd gone with Jake my emotions, my body, my spirit were overtaken by the sensation of an incombustible arson: intolerable conflict. At length I married the first man I got involved with.'

'And it hasn't worked out?' asks Ash, stepping carefully out of the bath, pulling a towel off the rail.

Beth still pours the bath water from one hand to the other. She shrugs.

'I don't know. This break may be final, or this may be a respite. Here, staying with you. An interval, and then perhaps, a fresh start with Theron.'

'Yes,' Ash agrees, 'it is the same with me.' Beth stretches out in the bath, her unshaven armpits are soapy.

'Will Jake come here after you?' she asks casually.

'No, no, he won't try that. He'll find enough to keep him happy. He'll manage.'

'And your children?'

Ash slips on a dark blue towelling robe with a purple border.

'They'll be OK,' she says carelessly, 'we have an au-pair cum nanny, she's very reliable, we left her in charge of them earlier this year for several weeks, while Jake and I were in the States. She'll manage until the autumn.'

'The autumn,' queried Beth, sitting up suddenly, with a sharp emphasis on the first syllable of the word autumn.

'Yes,' says Ash, not looking at Beth. 'Yes. By the autumn I'll have decided what to do. Hey, you'd better get out of the bath now, Beth. The water's getting cold.'

'OK.'

Beth stands up and pulls the plug out of the bath. Ash wraps a warm towel around her.

'You get finished up here and I'll go down and make us a quick lunch.'

Alone in the bathroom Beth wipes the steam from the mirror and says goodbye to her reflection.

After they've eaten and done the dishes, Ash opens the back door. Beth stands beside her on the threshold and the rainy air drenches them both. They feel they are standing by a waterfall and are invigorated. The slight tension that had remained between them, scraping their skins roughly, recedes, and their gestures again become gentle.

'I love the rain,' says Ash, 'it makes all my flesh as sensitive as the quicks beneath my fingernails.'

Their first real journey through the house begins in the kitchen and as they go through each room in the house, remembering the events that happened at various times in the rooms, they relive their first summer by a series of almost formal questions.

'Do you remember the first night I came to your room?' asks Beth, shyly, as they enter the little back bedroom. Ash's only answer is a smile.

In the bedroom with the yellowy faded wallpaper where Jake had slept, the women are silent, over-dosed with memories.

In the junk-room they try on costumes, giggling.

By the airing-cupboard they embrace, quickset women.

On the landing, Ash says in a shaky voice, 'will you release me from my captivity, Beth?'

Beth stares at her.

'Will you release me from mine, Ash?'

In the straggly light of a rainy afternoon, Ash turns and looks at Beth wordlessly.

'I will try to release you, my love,' says Beth hoarsely, 'I will...'

Before I came here to meet Ash, Beth thought, my throat was sore because I had been considering only one side of the problem of our relationship. Now when I wake Ash is next to me and her roots are delving deeply into me. That problem of mine: what is happening between me and Ash? makes more sense when I am with her. In isolation it frightened me. Now we are together it is the naturalness of us that strikes me most powerfully. With Ash I am no longer pretending. And I do not have to think of Vellet. The ghost cannot bring her quicksands here.

The girls have dragged the old mower out of the greenhouse

this afternoon and are taking it in turns to mow the lawn. They laugh and pant, struggling with the heavy old machine, and the familiar and somehow multilingual odour of the cut grass roams in the air.

Later, in the twilight, Ash lights candles in the kitchen. Beth stands by the window and looks at the livid bank of night cloud moving rapidly across the sky.

The warren of the moon is part of the night, and Ash is pressing her hands down on Beth's shoulders surreptitiously.

Like the inhabitants of a small island, the women grow nervous at nightfall.

Daylight is their domain.

But at night the flowers droop in intolerant vases. Ash walks in the garden. Beth sits by the window in the candlelight, unable to smile. We will grow more used to the night, she thinks, I am sure of that. But her tongue aches.

In the second week in August, Ash and Beth are walking between the tall trees and their voices, low, sibilant, are like part of the mist rising from the valley.

It is early in the morning.

They are speaking of their respective husbands, recalling intimacies and hard times, comparing their experiences.

'Jake was always bad-tempered at weekends,' said Ash.

Sombre thoughts about men are present in the minds of the women today, and they speak of the riddles each woman discovered at the heart of her marriage.

'And they will swallow us up greedily,' exclaimed Ash angrily, turning to Beth, 'until their houses become uninhabitable to us.'

Beth slides her hand into the oven glove and lifts the lid of the casserole dish, sniffing the meaty aroma. She gives it a good stir and then, satisfied, she re-sets the oven's timer and goes swiftly from the kitchen down the three white-washed steps to the scullery. She inhales deeply here, breathing in greedily the damp smell from the hempen sacks of potatoes, the odour of earth clinging to the potatoes and to the gardening tools that she and Ash have been using for the reclamation of the flowerbeds.

The big white ghostly freezer clicks gently, going through its rhythm of electrical coldness, but Beth forgets about the frozen vegetables and opens the top half of the old-fashioned backdoor to lean on the edge of the lower door and peer out across the still-warm evening garden. Beyond is the green hill of the giant, the slope which discoverers climb when it is necessary for them to change, to transform themselves.

These reflections please Beth. She smiles, is rapt before the scene, turns her head from the hill and looks across the moorland, at the tiny far-off sheep in their heavy fleeces. Her gaze continues until she comes to the roofs and smoke from the chimneys in the village at the foot of the hill.

Between the world of the giant and the world she has found with Ash, Beth hesitates. Ash does not want to climb the hill of the giant. Beth has suggested they walk up that way several times but each time Ash got that secluded look on her face.

'I went up there once on my own, before you arrived,' Ash protested, 'I don't like the atmosphere of the giant, anyway . . . I get nervous there . . .'

So Beth did not urge a visit. She smiles, is relaxed for the first time in months. The holiday feelings delight her. Her life with Theron has dropped away from her, the burden gone. This August experiment, the refreshment of her body, the daily contact with Ash would have seemed, a few weeks ago, an unattainable fantasy. Now Beth revels in their adventure in the old house. She exists without past or future. It is the same for Ash. We are adding the finishing touches to ourselves, thinks Beth, we are almost complete. The network of our bodies, from retina to follicle, bone to eyelash, cannot be queried.

Ash's blue nightdress hurtles from north to south, arms billowing as the warm wind buffets the clothes of the women pinned up to dry. Ash stands at the bedroom window, watching her blue nightgown speculatively. I am happy, she whispers.

Ash and Beth sit on the bench by the garden gate, laughing at old jokes, reminiscing. Over the past three days, they have overcome their fears of giving their love to one another again and seeing it disregarded or mocked. Beth, especially, has decided to live in the moment as it grows, as the embryo in the womb must do. She clasps her arms around her shoulders and looks hard at Ash.

'Why, you've cut your hair,' she said in surprise, 'I hadn't really noticed it until now.'

'Yes,' said Ash, 'I had it cut short ages ago. Have an apple.'

She hands Beth an apple and Beth bites into the flesh of the apple.

'It was a windfall apple,' says Ash.

'It's nice,' mumbled Beth, her mouth full.

Next morning, Ash took Beth's car and drove down to the village to do the shopping.

'I think it's better if I go alone,' she pointed out to Beth, 'no one will recognize me down there.'

'Theron might . . .' began Beth nervously.

'Then I'll worry about that when it happens, OK. Bye!'

Beth waved as the car disappeared down the lane.

Theron, she thought uneasily, I know where you are. You are at the other end of all the telephones. The 'phone box at the end of the road is where you live. When the strong summer wind gusts, the 'phone box door blows open and stays open. I have a strong urge to slip inside the red kiosk, to close myself in the small red building, lift the 'phone and speak to you. I know where you are. But I turn away from the temptation. I will not call you. You know where I am. Come and find me, if you want. Christ, I know your trick. Letting her cool off, you'll call it, that's what you'll say to yourself, when you sit in the summerhouse, a cigarette in your mouth, waiting for Vellet. While I am living with Ash, our life of sunlit reflections, you are living with the dark mirror of Vellet, dark, underwater, dead.

Beth pours herself a cup of coffee and settles herself in the windowseat to read through a batch of magazines, five years old. But it is her own story she reads, not the print on the garish pages. This is the story of the summer when the giant's mirror held out life to me. And I picked out what I wanted, from the reflections I was offered. As if plucking silky flags from a conjurer's shiny top hat. Here is the reflection I chose then: Ash. The lasting reflection.

Beth lets the magazine slip to the floor.

What about the other reflections I chose: what have I done with them? From the mirror I picked out moon, clock, menhir, leaf, arrow, star, sun, bee, candle and Ash. Ash, from whom I draw strength, who draws strength from me. When our bodies touch and embrace, we are learning all that our skins have to tell us, these soft rinds that cover flesh, bone and blood. We contemplate one another and discover we are new women. We compare notes, and reshape ourselves accordingly. I have plunged down into the depths of Ash these past few days, this is what I have longed for, and what I have always needed. The sympathy which existed between us, in miniature, as it were, has flowered and blessed us now. Does it matter now that I have lost or sold the other reflections, given them away, squandered them?

In that mirror long ago I saw the fountain of my life. As I stared I wanted to sleep but I was not allowed to sleep. The fountain swayed and began to flow over me, silver water and red blood, moonlight and seeds, and in the water I saw the face of Ash. I saw the face of Ash and I did not speak. The menhir taught me silence. I saw the face of Ash and I bled: the moon bandaged me. I saw the face of Ash and leaves burst from my body. I saw her, the fountain of my life. My companion.

Flaxen shadows flickering, curving.

Afternoon, and the bare flank of Ash's body, the freckled arms of Beth. The women are stretched out on a rug on the lawn, sunbathing. In an hour's time the first gnats of the evening will appear and drive the women indoors, squealing and slapping their flesh, but at the moment there is no flaw in their relaxation.

Their bodies are brown from the reflections of the sun. It is over a month since the morning of Beth's arrival and after the rain of that first day the days have been clear and hot, enabling the women to spend most of their time in the garden, happy tenants regardless of the length, long or short, of their stay.

But the weather breaks.

With a flick of a finger against thumb, Beth comes indoors, out of the rainy garden.

'Your hair! Your clothes! You're soaking wet!' cries Ash.

'Summer rain,' said Beth, 'It'll do no harm.'

Ash put out a hand and touched Beth tentatively, she touched her where her nipple showed against the wet cloth of her blouse. Ash looks shy and blushes.

'You look beautiful, Beth, all wet,' she whispers.

Outside, the rain runs off the sword-shaped leaves. Ash presses herself against Beth, against Beth's wet clothes. She is flushed, her tongue flicks against Beth's lips, her throat, her hands knead the damp cloth of the skirt she is pulling tight aross Beth's buttocks.

'I'll call you Cloacina today,' gasps Ash.

On the stairs, she strips Beth of her wet clothes, leaves them lying in a heap on the landing.

Beth is straining tight against Ash, she is alert for all Ash's instructions.

Ash is shivering in the warm room and web-like blotches appear on her skin, especially noticeable on her breasts.

She pushes Beth on to the unmade bed and stands at the foot of the bed, watching her, then watching herself in the mirror as she struggles with the husks of her clothes, pulling her bra and pants off. Still looking in the mirror, she parts her pubic hair and strokes herself. She looks over her shoulder at Beth, who is sitting up on the bed, and smiles coolly at her. Beth can see that Ash's clitoris is swollen and rigid. A pang goes through her own body. She scrambles forward off the bed and kneels before Ash. Bending her head she tastes Ash, her tongue roves against the taut projection of flesh and laps against the warm open cunt. Ash moans and shifts her weight to stand with her legs more widely astride, leaning her arms against the mirror. Beth uses her tongue to make Ash writhe and she can feel Ash's clitoris swell even more, like a delicate bulb. Beth's tongue is rotating faster and the pathway of Ash's vagina is alight, swirling with furnace sensations. The whole of her body presses against Beth's tongue until with an ache that pinches and floods her Ash comes and relaxes against the wall. Beth helps her to the bed and they lie down.

After a few moments, Ash slides her hand up Beth's leg.

'No,' says Beth, shyly.

But Ash can feel her quivering and she slides her finger cautiously up Beth's cleft. Beth is wet inside and she moves her finger slowly up and up until Beth groans and spreads her legs to give Ash more room to manoeuvre. Ash rubs Beth very slowly until her cunt was like strawberries crushed and mixed with cream and she was sweating and laughing and humping her behind until Ash brought her off just as Beth turned her head to stare at Ash fixedly and fiercely. She came, superhuman, with a wrenching orgasm, and collapsed into sleep like a star.

'This morning when I was in the village doing our shopping,' said Ash, 'a young man with longish blonde hair and old but clean clothes stopped me in the street and said, clearly and simply, "Will you give me a shilling to get something to eat?" '

Beth looks up from her book, startled.

Ash nods. 'Yes, strange, isn't it?' Beth looks at Ash and is afraid for her safety. She sees threats, pain, injury.

'He didn't menace you?'

'No, oh no. He was quite gentle.'

'What did you do?' asks Beth.

'I looked into his unstarving eyes and at his healthy body. I asked him, "how long since you've eaten?" He smiled sweetly and told me, "a long time." '

Ash is silent, lost in thought.

'And?' asked Beth impatiently.

'And what?'

'Did you give him any money?'

'Yes. Yes, I did.'

'I think you were foolish,' Beth told her quietly.

'Perhaps,' said Ash lightly.

'He didn't follow you home? We don't want him here, that sort.'

'Don't fuss, Beth. I'll never see him again, he was on the road, bumming around.'

'You liked him,' said Beth angrily.

'Maybe I did.'

Ash got up and began to brush her hair.

'Maybe I did like him,' she repeats, 'I am ashamed that I hesitated before giving him the money. I should have given it to him without shame. Perhaps he was laughing at me, perhaps it was a dare. But perhaps he was simply hungry.'

Beth snorts. 'You're a fool, Ash. You're too easily taken in.'

Ash puts down the brush and leans across the table towards Beth, speaking distinctly.

'But Beth, perhaps he had left all his friends and gone off alone by himself, and discovered that hunger was the worst part of loneliness?'

'Perhaps,' says Beth doubtfully.

'I think he was brave to beg, I was the one ill-at-ease, graceless, embarrassed. Why was I shocked, Beth?'

'I would have been shocked also,' said Beth, 'and perhaps refused to help at all.'

'Why are we so conditioned, so incapable of spontaneity, lacking any trust? Why do we hesitate to open our purses? The fuller our purses are, the tighter we close them, keep them closed.'

Beth remembers one time when she sat on the hilltop, spilling the dirty coins in her lap.

'Yes,' she whispers, 'those of us with purses full of money, we have most to learn.'

Beth stares at the flowers in the vase on the windowsill, blood-red flowers. She gets up from the table carefully, and goes upstairs to the lavatory.

Ash sits in the kitchen alone, letting her cup of coffee get cold, thinking of the beggar, the boy, his gaze.

'Wait!' said Ash, in that moonblue twilight.

'What is it?'

'Ssh! Over there!' warns Ash. 'I thought I saw someone in the shadows, over there.'

'I see no one,' says Beth. 'No one. No beggar, no ghost.'

Nervously, hand in hand, the women approach the patch of shadow at the side of the greenhouse.

'You see,' said Beth, 'there is no one, only the shadows.'

After a night of heavy rain, the deep and glowing colours of the garden amaze them. They stand at their bedroom window, exclaiming at the beauty of the day.

After breakfast, Ash peels the potatoes. It is her turn today. Beth watches her in silence for a while then she says,

'Sometimes, Ash, in the past, I longed either to be you, or to wipe you from the face of the earth, obliterating all memories of you.'

'Did you?' said Ash calmly, smiling.

'Yes. Your image on the few snapshots I had and cherished gave me pain. But now, these last weeks, all that lockjaw has gone. In the past I looked into the mirror and spat at my reflection. Now I can bear to look at it, and beyond, and can bear whatever comes to us, the long separations that no doubt we'll have to accept, the verdicts of our husbands and friends, the reunions in the future, you and I back here together again, the salvaged times. Angry shouts from the wilderness of men will try to wear out the strength of our womanhood, Ash, your children will summon you back with their cries, their demands, but we will survive it all.'

'Yes,' Ash replied, still peeling potatoes, 'we will survive, Beth.'

Afternoon, like a hand-held mirror, flashing, sparkling light.

The two women are out walking on the moor, rambling with no destination in mind.

Vellet looks at the giant and calls him by his first name. The giant cracks his knuckles and laughs. Often in the sickness of her limbo Vellet has planned to hunt the giant down. Vellet looks at the baby through a magnifying glass. She sees the yellowness of Jupiter and night comes ashore and her embroidered wings shiver.

'Do you see the two women, Vellet?' asked the Giant mockingly.

'I see them,' said Vellet shortly. 'Yes, I see them.'

The giant's eyes are open all night. His mirror is approaching the full.

'So, you have seen the two women, have you?' he says to Vellet, teasing her.

'Yes!' she exclaims, 'but I can't get near them, you know that. There's no place there for me. But what I want more than anything is rest. I want to sleep . . .'

Vellet, the sleepless ghost.

'I want to sleep,' she cries again, 'and to get away from the bar-

barism of my existence. What is holding me back? Why can't I break out of this orbit? Why can't I look into your mirror, Giant? I know the answer is there.'

'One day, after toiling hard,' answered the giant, 'you will have finished your tasks, Vellet.'

'When?' she asks eagerly, 'when?'

Long past midnight but hardly dawn yet. A hot summer night, a night that is not dark, where a perpetual twilight has taken the place of the dark. The moon is full, the moonlight reels about the lawn, the moorland; the moon is reflected in the glass of the greenhouse.

The two women sit on the lawn on the rug, wrapped in shawls. They have been drinking white wine since early evening and are conversing drowsily now, tipsy but not drunk.

Ash touches Beth and lets her hair loose into the moonlight.

'Jake's smile was becoming the smile of a collector of birds' eggs. I had to get away, Beth.'

Beth lies on her stomach, her cheek resting on her folded arms.

'And you, Ash, what were you becoming?'

'I? I was becoming the wife. A background, no more. A healthy young mare, unregarded as anything else.'

Beth turns over and stares up at the sky, the filmy boneless clouds. She has not said anything to Ash about Vellet. That has no place here. Beth will not bring the matter into this garden.

'I always liked Theron though,' drawled Ash, 'A bit dull perhaps, but decent. I expect it is different, being married to him.'

'Yes,' said Beth absently, 'It is, yes.'

Ash glances at Beth and decides to allow the events of the night to take their natural course. She is happy. Beth is happy. They need use few words. They are suckling each other back to strength. Love is shining softly between them. This is the Lammas month we were not wise enough to experience those years ago, thinks Ash, now we are able to accept our feelings for one another without shame, without peril.

'We are sharing the night, Beth.'

Beth nods slowly.

TWENTY SIX

NOT hand in hand, Beth and Ash are walking across the field of knee-high grass and buttercups. From the direction of the village comes a chime of bells. It is Sunday. The clang of bells reminds Beth of bones, teeth, keys. She glances at Ash, who is intent on picking her way, bare-legged, through the rough thistly ground. Beth is thinking about the past month of unhaunted days and nights with Ash. Beth and Ash pay one another homage, yet are careless as adolescents, giggling at their own shadows. Now in the pre-storm hush, under the dull sky that is tight with thunder, buzzing with electricity, the two women walk slowly, suddenly tired-out. Beth feels that her lips are swollen, that her expression has grown ugly. She notices that Ash is frowning at her, and then speaks to Beth with a new vigilance.

'We love each other, Beth. Beneath the foundations of our separate lives that love is our strength, the source of our energy. But we cannot isolate ourselves forever. From now on our meetings, our holidays' (she smiled here) 'will be frequent, we shall meet here in this house where we first recognized our affinity. I shall come alone, or sometimes, if you permit it, with the children. The house will be our sanctuary. But we have responsibilities elsewhere and cannot abandon those. I've refreshed myself here, at a time in my life when I thought there was no possibility of refreshment; I found the part of myself that was lost, the other side of me that you represent and reflect back to me. But if we stay together, you and I, we will stifle what we have. Do you agree? We have come to the end of our discoveries, for this visit. We must go back to the others in our lives, take our good news back. Do you agree?' she asks again, touching Beth's shoulder lightly.

Beth nods.

'Yes, Ash, I agree. After this month nothing will be the same again. We shall never lose sight of one another again. We are stronger now, stronger than we believed possible. And we must take our strength back into the world, and resume our places. We can re-animate our old lives.'

'That is what we must do.'

Now Beth and Ash run for cover, they shelter in the hedgerow. The storm is breaking. There is no lightning. Only the ache of thunder, and then the syllables of summer rain.

On the first day of September, Beth and Ash stand by the garden gate. It is a dark deaf morning. The women are quenched by yesterday's storms. Clouds exhaust the sky. When Beth mentions the giant, Ash is at first angry, then silent.

The women are on edge, the time of leave-taking is here.

The lawn the two women are crossing slowly seems, to Beth, to be pitted with craters. The colour of Ash's mood is red, the heart of a harp. Beth's colour is black, black as the flea's shadow.

Indoors, they cover the furniture with dust-sheets, the bed is stripped, the garbage packed in a black polythene bag and set by the gate-post for the dustmen to collect tomorrow morning. The house is returned to its solitude.

Ash's suitcase stands in the hall.

There is a hesitation in the women's speech. Now the time has come, they want to be far away from here, very quickly.

'We'll write, of course,' says Beth, 'and phone.'

'Yes,' murmurs Ash, and fidgets with her shoulder-bag. She is acting hardbitten. It is the only way she can survive. She stares at Beth arrogantly.

'We are right to do things like this,' she says loudly.

'Of course,' says Beth, opening her eyes wide.

The taxi blares its horn and Ash pulls the front door open violently, she lunges down the path with her case, Beth following behind.

The taxi driver puts the case in the boot of the car.

'Goodbye, Ash,' says Beth with composure.

Ash looks round the garden, up at the house, at Beth . . . She looks scared.

'Don't worry,' says Beth compassionately, 'don't worry.'

Ash smiles, relaxes, leans forward and kisses Beth, then gets into the car.

Beth bites her tongue. She is alone in the garden. The sky is without energy, is grey and stony.

Ash, Ash . . . She cannot imagine how she will be able to leave the house, with its many impressions of Ash, the hundred reflections, the cup Ash drank from, the knife she peeled apples with, her traces everywhere.

Depression, heavy and sour, is settling on Beth as she enters the house but her concentration is broken by a woman's cry.

Beth wheels round about to say, Ash! But instead she sees, very faint in the dull light, Vellet standing a few yards behind her.

Vellet has a joyful expression on her face.

She looks like the Virgin, thinks Beth, and does not dare to move.

Vellet stares at Beth, yet does not approach.

'Yes, I see what love is, Beth, I see it now. You and Ash, coming together, parting, planning to meet, involving others in your love, taking no selfish course, binding no one. Yes, I see. I can look into his mirror, now, look deeply into the mirror. Yes, and in the mirror of the giant, I see what I could never perceive before: love moving between all of us like fine weather, like a good moonrise, renewing us; like warm blood in our veins. I see far beyond the struggle for small rewards, possessions and territories, beyond the struggle that has kept me in one place for so long. Ah Beth, I am dissolving in this witnessed reflected love . . .'

Beth sees that Vellet's fingertips, breasts, eyelids are beginning to turn misty, an ectoplasm, the last of the ghost.

'The pangs of my ghosthood are erased,' whispers Vellet, 'and I open out into a hemisphere of water and light, blood and warmth and oh how easy it is, how easy, how simple at last, the freedom, I am lifted from my prison, I am on a new pathway, I see, I see . . .'

As the figure of Vellet fades wafting into this misty exhalation, Beth darts forward and cries,

'Vellet, wait, tell me . . .'

'Yes,' answers Vellet faintly.

'Vellet, will you follow Theron any more, will you haunt him again?'

A light and calm laughter.

'No, Beth, I will not haunt him any more. You can tell him, Beth, I forgive him for murdering me, it is of no importance now ... I am on this new pathway that I have seen in the mirror of the giant, that moon-mirror held up for me to look into, and I go down into a necessary dark, Beth, a dark redolent of the half-remembered smells of womb and atom. I am set free and I see my new reflection, my new beginning. I am ...'

The mists of the ghost disperse. There is only the grey and solid morning. Beth walks cautiously towards the spot where Vellet vanished. The air tingles but there is no other indication of anything out of the ordinary.

Now I must help Theron bear the loss of his haunting, thinks Beth. And all the time the knowledge of Vellet's transformation thrills through her. Such knowledge cannot be left behind, forgotten. It will always nourish my life, thinks Beth, for now I know Ash and I belong together, like twins, reflections, for our love freed Vellet. She enters the house gladly now, able to relish the touch and smell and aura of Ash that inhabits the house.

TWENTY SEVEN

HE is lonely.

Sometimes he sees all objects turning red.

I am afraid of blushing, he thinks.

It is a chilly evening and he would like to shun the garden. But by half-past six he can wait no longer and walks briskly across the lawn and into the summer-house.

There are autumn leaves on the summer-house floor.

Worth less than my good name, he thinks, scuffling the leaves with his feet.

He sits down to wait for his visitor.

He is ashamed of himself but cannot break the habit of coming to this place most nights.

My excrements frighten me, he thinks.

He can smell autumn forming in small drops in the air. He misses Beth badly. He would like her to come back. She is up at her old house, I know. But I'm not going after her. Let her come back here.

He wishes she would.

It is as if his loneliness is draining him of blood. His visitor is late tonight. Theron's body feels dull, slow-witted. Perhaps I have called the night by the wrong name, he thinks. A tiny animal of the arachnid class scuttled along the seat. He watches it, grimaces.

The dampness of autumn has entered the summerhouse. He can smell the fungus growing in the corner.

Where is Vellet? Although Vellet is unhappy, he feels no pity for her. He knows he is using her, but that is her tragedy.

He gets up and stands at the door. He looks up at the burr of the moon, at the thick shrubs of the garden. The mass of the house is grey and quiet. Theron would like the night to smell of acrobats and clowns but it is scented only with tomorrow's rain.

He saw Vellet coming towards him across the lawn, and he starts forward to greet her.

But Vellet wears on her head a hollow silver horn, rearing itself upward obliquely from her forehead.

She whispers, 'Theron, I am in deep water now, but I shall not drown . . .'

'Vellet,' he calls, but she's gone, leaving him steeped in silence.

The night is thinking deeply about Theron.

His laughter brays out across the garden. He is gaunt, there are loops of wire twisted around his heart and he hears Janus calling loudly. Will a man's nativity emerge from the flames of Theron? There is a fishhook caught in each of his ten fingers. He continues to resist the shadow of his sex. He is nailed to the threshold of the summerhouse, as if it were a leprosarium. It is as if I have half-forgotten some secret, some vital information, and my life depends on the recovery of this secret. He walks up and down the lawn.

'Am I haunted?' he asks out loud, 'or has the ghost abandoned me?'

'Vellet has gone,' Beth answers softly, 'Vellet has begun her next journey.'

Beth is walking towards him, from the shadow of the house.

'Why has she gone,' asks Theron resentfully, 'and where?'

Beth does not answer. She stands beside Theron, who does not touch her, moves a little away, stiffly.

'It was you and Ash!' he shouts suddenly, 'You two have driven Vellet away!'

Again Beth does not answer. She shook her head and walked towards the summerhouse, leaving Theron to gather his thoughts. He is as deep in thought as if calculating the moon's age.

Smiling to herself, Beth sits in the dark summerhouse. Theron stood in the doorway and asked,

'Will I see Vellet again?'

'No, never,' said Beth quietly, not moving, not looking at him.

Then the questioner approaches her and she looks up at him, smiling and gentle. She takes his hands and shows him how to celebrate the riddance of the ghost. She shows him the pinnacles of her body, with its new confidence gained from loving Ash, she takes him further than Vellet into the burning cascades, further into the woman, she loves him until he begins to sing with the vision of it, descending into the hollows of her body, gaining his freedom, his independence.

The lovers have gone beyond emergencies. A new partnership has begun. Now the roots and branches of Beth and Theron twine together and whatever storms attack them will not easily despoil their growing landscape.

TWENTY EIGHT

As they walk by the river in the late afternoon, Beth says to her husband,

'All over the world, men and women are longing for peace.'

Theron nods. 'It is true,' he said.

'We are free of the ghost,' said Beth wonderingly. The autumn evening is a gauzy cupboard within which thin flowers blow.

Theron is growing accustomed to the place Ash has in Beth's life now. He is no longer jealous. He finds the matter strange. Strange, exciting. Last weekend, on the phone, Jake had said to him, 'can't you stop Beth interfering with Ash and me?' Theron had laughed and said, 'does Ash want Beth to stop interfering?' After Theron's long affair with Vellet, he finds in himself a sympathy with unorthodox love.

When Vellet left him, when the pressure of guilt and ghost lifted from Theron, he'd felt even lonelier at first. He realized his dependence on Vellet, was both ashamed and proud of it. She was like an elixir, he thinks, and I move less agilely without her. When I make love to Beth, I think of Vellet sometimes. But less often. My memory of Vellet gets thinner each day and night. I am full of hope for the future and I love Beth. I accept the exodus of Vellet. Ash is part of Beth's life and therefore part of mine. When I come to the end of my loneliness, the time when I never think of Vellet, then I too will be able to grasp the extent of my good fortune.

Beth is thinking of Ash's letter. 'I was so happy ... all that month ... I think Jake will see the sense in it eventually, accept it as Theron does, that you and I experience the love, and more, of sisters ...'

On his hill, the giant is silent. His white silhouette is frail as autumn frost.

Theron sighs, a long audible breath. There is no mirror for him yet. Beth glances at him, determined to resolve any existing difficulties in their life. For we are still composed of dangerous elements.

'What are you thinking?' she asks quietly.

'Of Vellet,' he answered at last. 'Sometimes, in the evening, I think of Vellet. She is a component of my twilight depression. Alone in the house sometimes, too, I think of her.'

'It is natural,' said Beth, 'there will be some trace left for a while. But we have whole years before us without the ghost.'

Theron turns to her gratefully and touches her body, breast and stomach. There is my mirror, he thinks suddenly. Our unborn infant is in his warm water laboratory, growing fast, unstoppable.

Theron kisses Beth. He does not want to solve anything. He is perfectly happy with the gleam of his thoughts, the ease of his heartbeat. It is as if a blindness caused from many hours of adoring flowers has dropped from him and he sees Beth welcoming him. He kisses Beth again.